Scandal School
Sex Tape

by Cat Cavaleri

Published by Obelus Division
ISBN: 978-1-7320784-9-9

Contents

Scandalicious News

Logan Asher Wyatt, the infamous rich-boy car thief, is missing!

By Margot York

Remember Logan Asher Wyatt? Of course you do!

We all saw the viral videos captured by witnesses to last month's shocking car crash. Who could forget the sight of 14-year-old Logan being dragged to a waiting police vehicle by not one, not two, but six cops, as he screamed the immortal words at the top of his lungs, "Do you know who my father is?!"

As a matter of fact, Logan, your friends at *Scandalicious News* know exactly who your father is. He's Richard Asher Wyatt, heir to the billionaire Wyatt family's vast fortune. Our tireless reporters enjoyed the amenities of several Wyatt-owned airlines, hotels and fast food chains while staking out your family's massive estate during your bond hearing for grand theft auto…and involuntary manslaughter.

As we reported last month, the Notorious L.A.W. got off with a paltry fine and a ding on his juvenile record for the horrific accident that totaled his neighbor's 1.2-million-dollar Lamborghini 400 GT and put a tragic end to the life of the reckless teen's passenger, 15-year-old prep school student Edwin Fraser Vandenberg.

Read all about how Logan partied it up with his pals after getting off with an outrageously light slap on the wrist **here** (including a **SHOCKING SLIDESHOW!)**

But now, Logan is missing!

Just hours after *Scandalicious News* uploaded our **EXCLUSIVE EXPOSÉ** on little Logan's long history of naughty behavior, America's wealthiest hooligan vanished right out from under everyone's noses.

Nobody, including our confidential sources within the Wyatt household, have a clue where he is.

There's nothing the powerful Wyatt family hates more than scandals. Where are they hiding young Logan?

You can count on *Scandalicious News* to find out!

Chapter 1

"So," said the woman to the girl. "You made a sex tape. With one of the most powerful men in the United States. And you're sixteen."

"Seventeen," the girl replied.

"Oh, seventeen, my mistake," the woman said, consulting the papers in the plain manila file that lay on her desk. "That makes *such* a difference."

She gave the girl a smile. It was sly and malicious.

"Girl, age seventeen…no name?" the woman continued, rustling through the papers. "Well, many children arrive at our school with no names. Anonymity is our primary objective, after all."

The girl shifted uneasily on the hard wooden chair. She glanced down at the school uniform—gray wool skirt, navy blazer, and purple necktie with diagonal yellow stripes—which she had donned moments after she arrived in this strange place. She felt dazed.

She had absolutely no idea where she was.

"I'm not a child," the girl said.

The woman closed the file and eyed her. The girl squirmed.

Hours ago—twelve, twenty-four, maybe as many as forty-eight—the girl had been shopping at the mall a few miles from her home. By the time she finished it was very late and the mall was closing. As she stepped out of the elevator and into the deserted parking garage, she heard a shrill squeal of tires coming from the lower level. Suddenly, a black van with no windows pulled to a stop in front of her, blocking her path. The back door flew open, and before she could do more than freeze in shock, a pair of men wearing black ski masks leaped out, seized her, and forced her inside.

"Don't scream," one of them said, as the other covered her eyes with a blindfold. It wasn't a makeshift scrap of cloth, but a device designed for professionals, expertly constructed with sturdy nylon straps, adjustable clasps, and a locking mechanism that clicked into place as he fit it around her head.

"Be a good girl. If you struggle, we'll tie you to the seat," a third voice barked as rough hands forced her to sit and the van door slammed. Then the engine revved and they sped away.

For all intents and purposes, it had been a violent kidnapping. Except for one thing.

She had expected it. She submitted to it willingly.

The van drove for countless miles. Her abductors refused to say a word in response to her increasingly agitated questions. She grew weak from spent adrenaline. She got very hungry. Her thoughts became muddled. Maybe she dozed.

Then all at once, the van came to a halt. She heard the door open. She tried to ask what was happening, but her words were transformed into a strangled shriek as unseen hands grabbed her and yanked her out of her seat. Instinctively she began to flail her arms and kick her legs as her abductors lugged her out of the van, dragged her across ground that felt like asphalt, and shoved her into...something.

"Don't move," a voice commanded.

She huddled on a hard surface covered with rough carpet, unable to see a thing through the blindfold. Somewhere very close, a powerful engine growled to life. Then a violent rushing sensation struck her and she felt her stomach drop as she ascended into the air.

A plane. She was in a small plane.

Was she alone? Or were her captors with her? Tentatively, she reached out and felt around the space, but her fingers contacted only coarse carpet and cold, smooth walls. She could feel no seats, no windows, nothing at all. She scrabbled at the clasps and straps of her blindfold, tugging and tearing at them, but they refused to budge.

After a long flight, the aircraft began to descend just as swiftly as it had ascended. Her stomach clenched queasily as it landed with a bump. She heard the sound of a door opening, then she shivered as crisp air rushed into the cabin.

It was clean, thin air. High-altitude air.

Blunt fingers slipped over her head and worked the clasps of her blindfold. It fell away and light dazzled her eyes. She squinted in pain as afternoon sunlight, filtered through gauzy clouds, filled her vision. Someone took her gently by the arm and guided her out of the plane. As her feet met solid ground and her eyes adjusted, she gazed around her in astonishment.

She was in a valley. Towering mountains reared overhead, stretching their snow-capped peaks impossibly high, as if trying to pierce the exquisite blue sky and its drapery of hazy clouds. She was standing on a small landing strip at the southern end of the valley. It extended like a trench for several miles to the north, where it tapered into a tight, impassible corridor through the mountains. At the center of the valley were rolling green pastures, flaxen haystacks, and small red barns. At the point where the steep walls of bare rock came together beyond the farmland, she could just make out a sparkling lake.

To the east and west, a near-vertical rockface loomed above the verdant valley floor. On one side, there was a town filled with small cottages, quaint shops, and a well-kept park. On the other, there was a school.

It was an enormous, grand school with a soaring gothic façade of gray stone, many-paned windows that glinted in the afternoon sun, and an eight-foot-high brick wall that fully surrounded both the structure and its grounds. Within the wall, she could see stables for horses, a soccer field, and an impeccably maintained lawn. Dozens of figures were moving to and fro on the grass.

Kids.

"Let's get you changed," a voice murmured in her ear.

The girl flinched, then turned to see one of the kidnappers standing at her side. She was maskless, her expression neutral.

"Aren't you worried that I've seen your face?" the girl asked.

"Doesn't matter," the kidnapper replied. "You'll never see it again after today."

She took the girl by the arm and led her into a small outbuilding that abutted the landing strip. Lying neatly folded on a simple wooden table were a gray wool skirt, a navy blazer, a white blouse, black tights, and a purple tie with narrow yellow stripes. A pair of brown leather pumps stood beneath the table, the rounded toes pointing at her.

"Put these on," her captor ordered.

"Why?" the girl asked.

"Every student has to wear the school uniform. No exceptions."

The girl hesitated, then turned away and awkwardly removed her jeans, sweatshirt, socks, and sneakers. She pulled on the tights and skirt. She buttoned up the blouse. She cinched the tie into a clumsy knot around her neck. Everything fit perfectly, as if each piece had been made especially for her. The garments felt rich and luxurious against her skin, exactly like she imagined the most expensive designer clothes might feel. She'd never worn anything like them before in her life.

As she pulled on the blazer, her fingers brushed against an embroidered patch on the left lapel.

It was a school crest. It was shaped like a shield, with red and gold borders. At its center was a sinuous purple S that reared like a snake out of a deep blue field, its head rising into an area of lighter blue.

Now, half an hour later, she fingered the embroidered patch again and considered the woman seated behind the imposing desk. She was backlit by a tall window that was flanked by thick velvet curtains as green as damp moss. It was hard to look at her. The white-gold sunlight caught the silver threads in her black hair and made them glow like tiny bolts of lightning in a midnight sky. The girl shifted her eyes to the window. The view it afforded was of the equestrian grounds, and beyond them a wooded glen choked with evergreen trees and thick brush, and beyond that the precipitous gray rockface.

Where on earth was she?

The woman folded her hands on the manila file. She did not smile.

"Let me explain where you are and what you can expect," she said. "This is a boarding school. A very exclusive boarding school. Our students are special children facing unique... challenges."

"Challenges?" the girl said, crossing her arms. "You mean, they're all sluts like me?"

"I mean, they're all involved in scandals, like you," the woman said. "Scandals of their own making, such as yours. And scandals

6

they've inadvertently become caught up in. We offer privileged children, like yourself, a safe place to weather the storm, as it were. But…"

She flicked her eyes up and down the girl. She studied her for a painfully long time. The girl met her gaze. She tried not to blink, but after a moment she had to look away from the woman's piercing black eyes.

"You're not privileged, are you? Your high-powered political playmate is footing the bill. This is not unheard of here. It's not typical, though. As a girl from a modest background, you may feel that your peers are of a very…alien class."

"How do you know I'm not rich?" the girl said.

This made the woman laugh.

"Come now," she said, her voice bright with amusement. "It's painfully obvious. I'll caution you not to try to pull the wool over your classmates' eyes. It will only make things harder for you if they mark you as lower class *and* a liar."

The woman leaned back in her chair.

"This school is a hiding place," she continued. "It's completely off the grid. Inaccessible to the outside world. And that includes members of the media. Nobody will bother you here. No one will photograph you, or record you, or post updates about your whereabouts and actions. While you're with us, you will effectively disappear off the face of the earth. And those in the outside world will gradually lose interest in your scandal, forget about you, and move on to the next piece of shocking news."

"Are you the school principal?" the girl asked.

"I am the headmistress," the woman replied.

"How many kids are here?"

"Fifty-two. No, fifty-three, now that you're with us. We have the capacity for one hundred students, though we rarely accept so many. Our children come to us from a variety of countries. The majority are between the ages of fourteen and seventeen. We don't admit adults. Our youngest child right now is twelve. We rarely allow anyone younger than that. Though we once enrolled an infant in our school."

The girl blinked in surprise.

"What kind of scandal can a baby cause?"

"The baby *was* the scandal," the woman replied.

"What's your name?" the girl asked.

The woman shook her head.

"No names here. No real names, that is. That's rule number one. You will call me Headmistress. While you're with us, your name will be…" the headmistress considered her, then a calculating smile flashed across her face. "Beryl."

"Barrel?" the girl repeated. "Like what people kept whiskey in back in the olden days?"

"No. Beryl," the headmistress enunciated. "A gem of great rarity, great hardness and, when transparent, of great beauty. I wonder how transparent you'll prove to be in the coming weeks."

"Weeks?" the girl—Beryl now—repeated. "I'm going to be stuck here for weeks?"

The headmistress did not reply.

"How many weeks?" Beryl asked.

"Perhaps a few. Perhaps many."

"How many is 'many?'"

"Yours has the trappings of an uncommonly tenacious scandal. It may take several dozen weeks for it to blow over."

"You mean months? I might be here for *months*?"

"We don't measure time in months here. No calendars, no seasons. Just the school week. Monday through Friday, followed by the traditional weekend. We've found it to be better, psychologically speaking, for children. You'll get used to it soon enough. One thing, though."

The headmistress leaned across the desk, thrusting her face close to Beryl's with an aggression that made the girl instinctively recoil. The woman's lips curled up at the corners. It wasn't a smile but a snarl, like a tiger might give its prey.

"However long you end up spending with us, I hope to never hear your voice again once your stay comes to an end."

"What does that mean?"

The headmistress did not reply.

A shiver—involuntary and irrepressible—shook Beryl's body. She swallowed and glanced around the headmistress's office. The

8

hardwood floor was worn, but it had been waxed to a glass-like sheen. Here and there, faded oriental rugs added muted splashes of color to the space. The walls were lined with shelves crammed end-to-end with leather-bound books that looked old enough to belong in a museum. To the left of the desk and the bright window was a small door. Hung on it at eye-level was an antiquated engraving of an owl. The office looked like the private study of a nineteenth-century English academician.

But there were no valleys like this in England.

Were there?

"Where are we? I mean, where is this place?" Beryl asked.

"We're in a very safe, very secret location," the headmistress said. "I promise, no one can get in. And no one, *no one*, can get out."

"Are we in the United States? Europe? South America?" Beryl asked.

The headmistress simply gazed at her, a placid smile on her face. A patronizing smile. Beryl glared at her in response.

"I want to call someone," she said.

The headmistress opened one of her desk drawers, reached inside, and pulled out Beryl's phone. She held it up as if she were starring in a cell phone commercial and Beryl was the camera, then she cradled it in both hands and studied it.

"With this?" she said. "I see many, many phones arrive with our students. The latest models. Designs not available to the general public. But this is extremely unusual. I've never seen anything like it. I wonder how you got your hands on it."

"The senator gave it to me," Beryl said. "My 'high-powered political playmate,' as you called him."

"Ah," the headmistress replied. "That explains it. He's quite prominent in the intelligence community, isn't he? That would give him access to the latest technology. And spy gear, perhaps?"

She smiled craftily at Beryl, then placed the phone back in the drawer. She withdrew a key chain from the pocket of her jacket. It was an out-of-date jacket made of bright turquoise fabric, studded with brassy nautical buttons, and scaffolded by enormous shoulder pads. She held up the key for Beryl to see, used it to lock the drawer, and placed the key chain back in her pocket with a flourish.

"You can't do that!" Beryl protested. "He said I could call, and—"

"Rule number two," the headmistress said. "No communication with the outside world. No cell phones, no landline phones. No email. No social media. No internet. No letters or faxes or telegrams. No communication."

"No internet? Are you serious?"

"Do I look serious?"

Beryl eyed the headmistress's jacket.

"So, it's like we're trapped in the 1980s? Like your clothes?" she sneered.

"You ask an inordinate number of questions for a seventeen-year-old," the headmistress wryly noted. "Are you sure you're really a teenager?"

Beryl scowled.

"This sucks," she grumbled.

The headmistress reached out a finger. Beryl noted that the nail was long and heavily lacquered with retro red polish. More 1980s style. She used it to press a button on a smooth, tan box that sat on her desk wedged between a stack of files and a cup filled with pens. The box looked like an old-fashioned computer speaker, but twice the size. Through the closed office door, Beryl heard three distinct notes chime, then the headmistress's voice echoed down the hall as she spoke a brisk command.

"Poe. Come to the headmistress's office at once."

Poe was sitting in their least loved class: L&L. Language and literature. The summons was almost a relief.

Almost.

Mr. Lark turned away from the dingy intercom speaker mounted on the wall above the blackboard and gave Poe a nod.

"Go on," he said. "Hurry back when you're done. We'll be starting on the Percy Shelley poem after the quiz."

Poe had neither studied for the quiz nor read the poem. They had no intention of hurrying back. L&L was the last class of the day. They hoped the headmistress had a message for them to deliver or an errand for them to run that would take up the rest of the period. Sometimes she did. Poe was the only student she entrusted with such tasks.

Poe rose from their desk, exited the classroom, and pointed their footsteps toward the headmistress's office. It was a walk they'd made countless times, but it always filled them with a sense of dread.

Like they were in trouble.

Maybe they were. You could never be sure.

Poe climbed the creaky stairs to the third floor. L&L was on the second floor. The gym—actually, now that they thought about it, that was their least loved class—was on the ground floor. From behind the classroom doors, they could hear the murmuring hum of teachers lecturing and students responding.

The headmistress's door was firmly closed. That meant she was in there with a student. That, in turn, meant Poe hadn't been summoned because they'd committed some misdeed they hadn't been aware of. They let out a sigh of relief, raised their fist, and knocked.

"Come in," the headmistress called out. Her voice sounded cheery. Another good sign.

Poe grasped the tarnished brass knob, turned it, and pushed the door inward. Sure enough, there was a girl seated before the desk in the dreaded chair. Nobody liked sitting in the chair. It meant you were going to get it. When you weren't in trouble, the headmistress sat you down on the comfortable button-studded leather divan next to the door, while she lounged in the wingback chair across from you. Sometimes she gave you tea, if she was trying to trick you into tattling on one of your classmates.

But the girl seated in the chair wasn't in trouble. She was new.

Poe hesitated on the threshold of the office until the headmistress beckoned to them.

"This is Beryl. She will be with us for a time," said the headmistress.

It was what she always said. "With us for a time." Sometimes, that time was two weeks. Sometimes twenty. Sometimes two hundred.

"Take her to the dormitory and get her settled. Then bring her with you to Mr. Lark's class. She might as well start her daily routine right away."

"Which dorm room's she assigned to?" Poe asked.

"Yours."

"What?" Poe exclaimed.

"You're both juniors. You'll be rooming together."

Poe knew better than to protest, but they couldn't suppress the scowl that instantly compressed their brow or the resentful glare they shot at the new girl, who offered them a quick, apologetic glance.

"Why can't she room with Electra?"

"Because I want her with you."

Poe folded their arms over their chest and let out an irritable huff. The headmistress rose from her chair and crossed the room to Poe, who had come no farther into the office than the wingback chair and the divan. She quirked her finger and Poe obediently tipped their head up to give her a clear path to their ear.

Glancing at the girl, the headmistress bent down and whispered, "I want you to keep an eye on her for me. There's something strange about her. Very strange."

Poe gave the headmistress a grudging nod. It wouldn't be the first time they'd done this sort of thing for her. As tasks went, though, it was completely distasteful. Poe hated having a roommate.

"Beryl," the headmistress said brightly. "Meet Poe. They will show you around. Don't hesitate to ask them any questions you may have. Poe knows which ones they are allowed to answer."

The girl hesitantly stood up. She was short. Shorter than Poe by several inches, barely five feet tall. And pretty, in an unfledged sort of way.

"Come on," Poe grumbled, yanking the door open. "The dorms are in the south wing."

The two of them walked to the staircase in silence. The new girl—Beryl, the headmistress had said—trailed Poe by half a step.

"Your name's Poe?" she ventured at last as they descended, their hard-soled shoes clunking on the wooden stairs in noisy syncopation.

"It's short for Edgar Allan Poe. The author."

"Do people call you Edgar?"

"No. Just Poe."

"Is it your real name?"

"It's my school name."

"What's your real name?" Beryl asked.

"I'm not telling," Poe said.

"Do you want to know mine?"

"No way," Poe replied. "We're anonymous for a reason. Don't tell kids your real name. If anyone ever tries to tell you theirs, don't let them. Both of you will get in trouble."

"What kind of trouble?"

Poe looked at her grimly.

"You don't wanna find out."

At the far end of the second floor, the spartan wooden floors of the west wing gave way to the opulent ruby carpet of the south wing. The bare academic walls were replaced with polished wainscoting and intricately carved wall panels of deeply stained walnut. Easy chairs and benches upholstered in rich brocade, elegant end tables topped by lamps shaded with stained glass, and oil paintings of placid country scenes were scattered along the hall between the closed dorm room doors.

Poe halted in front of their door, opened it, and ushered Beryl inside.

"Here," they said, grouchily sweeping their clothes off the spare bed. "This one's yours. That closet and dresser are yours, too. Looks like your stuff's in them already."

Poe jerked a thumb to indicate the neatly hung navy blazers and gray skirts in the freestanding Georgian-style wardrobe on Beryl's side of the room. This new roommate clearly hadn't been a spur-of-the-moment whim on the headmistress's part. Maybe it was a punishment for something Poe didn't realize they did.

Poe sighed and tossed their clothes onto their own bed as Beryl peered into her closet, then into the drawers of her matching dresser.

"It's so weird," she said.

"What?" Poe said.

"How well this uniform fits."

"It's not weird," Poe said, a trace of irritation creeping into their voice. "It's bespoke."

"Be-what?" Beryl said.

"Custom made," Poe said. "By the tailor in town."

"Wow," Beryl said, shutting the wardrobe door. "I figured this was a hand-me-down from an old student, or something."

Poe snorted in disgust.

"That's idiotic," they said. "And gross."

"This place knows everything about me except my name," Beryl murmured to herself, then a look of alarm came into her eyes. "Wait. How did the tailor get my measurements?"

Poe just shrugged.

"It had to be before the kidnapping," Beryl said, her eyes darting around the room. "There wasn't enough time to sew a skirt, a jacket, and a shirt from scratch...was there?"

She stared at Poe. Terror crept into her face.

"Was there enough time?" she whispered. "How long ago was I grabbed?"

Poe shrugged again.

"What day is this?" Beryl demanded.

"Thursday."

"I mean, what's the date?"

Poe shrugged a third time.

Beryl grabbed their wrist. Poe wrenched their arm away. They didn't like being touched.

"What is the date? Tell me!"

The new girl's voice was becoming shrill. She was getting scared. This was normal: all the new kids acted like this when they realized they were trapped. Sometimes they cried.

"You ask a lot of questions. It's not a good idea here," Poe said.

"What is this place?" the girl swallowed hard and her eyes, though not yet wet, were beseeching. "I mean, what's it called?"

"It doesn't have a name," Poe said. "But we kids call it Scandal School."

Beryl's lower lip quivered. Poe rolled their eyes.

"Don't. We have to get to class. You can cry in the bathroom later. Never in here," Poe emphasized. "Especially not at night. I'm a light sleeper."

Chapter 2

Scandalicious News
Logan Asher Wyatt pees his way into another scandal

By Margot York

He's baaaaack! Two short years after Logan Asher Wyatt made headlines across the country for the appalling car crash that did tens of thousands of dollars of damage and tragically cut short the life of a promising young student, Logan's making headlines once again.

What did the country's wealthiest 16-year-old juvenile delinquent do this time?

It seems that two weeks ago, the Notorious L.A.W. got bored while on a five-star deluxe vacation with his family in New York City. Our Richie Rich wannabe appears to have been unaware that it's illegal to get wrecked on cocaine, break into a cathedral after dark, and urinate on holy ground in the Big Apple.

Actually, it's illegal *EVERYWHERE* in the good ol' U.S. of A., Logan!

According to *Scandalicious News's* anonymous source within the NYPD, upon being apprehended by local law enforcement, Logan unironically repeated the catchphrase that launched a million memes, "Do you know who my father is?!"

Unfortunately for our privileged prince, the punishment for doing coke, trespassing on Vatican-consecrated property, and vandalizing a sacred structure isn't a measly fine and a strongly worded reprimand — not when you're a 16-year-old repeat offender on probation.

It's prison time.

Maybe a little prison time ... no, make that a lot of prison time. But Daddy Wyatt wasn't having it. After Logan was released from Rikers Island on bail, he scooped up his boy, loaded him onto a private jet, and father and son fled to the swanky, heavily guarded Wyatt estate.

Logan was spotted on the property by *Scandalicious News* camera crews several times, usually talking on a cell phone, smoking, and looking awfully cocky for a teen with an involuntary manslaughter conviction in his sealed juvenile record. Check out this **EXCLUSIVE SLIDESHOW** of Logan haunting the grounds of the ostentatious Wyatt estate!

As we **reported two years ago**, Logan abruptly vanished following his first scandal. He quietly returned to his lavish life of pampering and parties after the buzz about him died down nearly a year later.

Well, surprise, surprise: Logan hasn't been seen in more than three days. Has he vanished once again?

Where did he go when he was 14? And is that where he's hiding right now?

Scandalicious News is on it!

"Two more minutes," Mr. Lark announced as he strolled the classroom, glancing over his students' hunched shoulders while they scribbled away in their notebooks. The fifteen questions of the quiz, written in white chalk on the blackboard at the front of the classroom, had clearly confounded Socrates, who was staring with numb bemusement at the blank page of his notebook. Darwin, meanwhile, had already finished and was doodling what Mr. Lark hoped was a rocket ship and not a male anatomical feature at the bottom of her neatly inked notebook sheet.

"One more minute," Mr. Lark said. "This shouldn't have been difficult, people."

He'd taken to calling his students "people" because, as the newest teacher in the school and the youngest at just twenty-four years of age, it felt wrong to call them "kids." He'd tried out "folks" for a while, but the term confused the non-native English speakers. There had been one disastrous attempt at "my friends," but it sounded so pompous to his own ears that he never used it again.

He refused to call them "children" as the headmistress did. Most of them were just seven years younger than him.

"Three…two…one…pens down, notebooks closed. Pass them up, you know the drill," he said as the ten students in his junior level language and literature class grudgingly handed their notebooks forward to the front row, where he collected them.

In any other school, the class would have been called "English." But with so many of his students hailing from non-English-speaking countries, he tailored his curriculum to cast as international an educational net as possible. Last week, they'd covered waka poetry from the Heian period of Japan. This week, it was the Romantic poets of nineteenth-century Europe. The abrupt transition of a thousand years and an entire continent had proved challenging for his newest students, Amethyst and Garnet (the headmistress was apparently on a mineral-naming kick lately), who spent the first three days of the week raising their hands in the middle of his lectures to ask, "Wait…so now the poems are *supposed* to rhyme?"

He'd been told to expect a new student today. A girl. He wondered if she'd be named Jade or Onyx. Maybe Lapis Lazuli.

He didn't have to wonder for long.

"Percy Bysshe Shelley," he said, taking up a tattered, cloth-bound book that had been printed in 1921. "Author of the poem 'To a Skylark,' one of my favorites for obvious reasons, which each of you should have read last night. 'All that ever was joyous and clear and fresh—thy music doth surpass. Teach us, sprite or bird, what sweet thoughts are thine.' Who can explain what Shelley meant the bird to represent in this passage of the poem? Anyone?"

With a creak, the classroom door opened and Poe entered. A girl trailed them uneasily. Every head swiveled to stare at her. A new student was by no means an unusual event, but it was always an interesting one.

"This is Beryl," Poe said in their blunt, perennially unamused voice.

"Beryl," he murmured under his breath. "Good name."

He assumed the welcoming smile he'd worn countless times: a kind but impersonal smile for students who arrived suddenly, and just as suddenly vanished, never to be seen again.

"I'm pleased to meet you, Be—"

His words dried up in his throat.

His eyes widened. His blood turned to ice water.

Astonished, he stared at the girl, who stood with her head lowered shyly.

He knew her.

Dear God, he *knew* her!

Like a punch to the gut, the memory knocked the wind out of him, paralyzed him, left him speechless.

They had met in an English classroom in the Outside world, just like this one. The late afternoon sun had leaked through the dusty windowpanes like molten copper, transforming the soft strands of her hair into red and gold flames, exactly like now.

She had just turned seventeen the day they met.

"By the way," he'd said, as he was packing up his books and papers, preparing to leave. "Happy birthday."

She'd smiled at him in surprise.

"How did you know it's my birthday?"

"I have my ways," he'd replied, smiling back at her.

The final bell had rung. The classroom was deserted. They were all alone.

They lingered for a quarter of an hour: he complimenting her report on Samuel Taylor Coleridge, she expertly steering the conversation back to him again and again and again.

Where did he live? What did he like to do for fun? Did he love writing as much as she did?

This was dangerous territory and he knew it. But he didn't put a stop to it until she leaned closer to him, placed her hand on his, and asked, "Do you have a girlfriend?"

He'd abruptly hoisted his bag, gave her an awkward wave, and said, "See you tomorrow. Hope you get lots of presents."

It was dangerous because he wanted to kiss her.

He desperately wanted to kiss her.

She followed him out of the school, past the deserted football field, and through the nearly empty faculty parking lot.

"Hey," she called out.

He should have kept walking. But he didn't. He stopped and turned around.

"I know about you," she said.

His heart stopped.

"What do you know?" he said, his voice unsteady.

"I know it's not your fault," she said.

He should have turned and walked away from her.

He should have turned and run away from her.

Instead, he took a step toward her.

Then another.

Then, they kissed.

That was the first time. There were many more times after that.

Mr. Lark blinked and swallowed hard, twice. It was impossible—how could she be here?

He swept his eyes over her face, a face he knew so well. She regarded him blandly.

She didn't recognize him. It made sense. He had grown a beard since the last time they saw each other. He'd changed his hairstyle. He was dressed very differently—academic-cut tweed jacket with elbow patches, light blue button-down shirt, brown trousers, yellow tie with thin purple stripes. It was the school-mandated uniform for teachers, light years from the style of clothes he'd preferred when he knew her.

He'd changed.

But she hadn't.

Not at all.

"Please," he croaked. "Take a seat."

With a hand that trembled spasmodically, he indicated an empty desk at the front of the class next to Saint Augustine, his worst student.

"Try to...to follow along," he said, as she slid into the seat. "We can talk later. I mean, about the classwork, that is."

He realized that he was staring openly at her. All ten of his students—no, eleven, now that Poe was back at their desk…no, twelve, now that this girl who was not named Beryl was here—all of them were unquestionably aware that he was staring at her.

"The image of the bird," he said, grabbing the book of poems and riffling through the pages with palpable desperation. "Free. Uncaged. Poe, please share your thoughts on this passage: 'Teach us, sprite or bird, what sweet thoughts are thine: I have never heard praise of love or wine that panted forth a flood of rapture so divine.'"

As Poe hemmed and hawed their way through an indirect admission that they were encountering the poem for the very first time, he glanced at the new girl.

Beryl.

That was no more her name than Lark was his.

Sensing his gaze, she raised her eyes from the surface of her desk.

They were unfocused. Disoriented. Exhausted.

They idly roved his face, and then, with a suddenness that made both of them flinch, a flash of recognition made them go wide.

Her gasp, clearly audible, sent a jolt through her body.

Her eyes delved into his. They were startled. Alarmed.

And very, very frightened.

They were exactly like his eyes.

Scandalicious News
Logan Asher Wyatt sought by the FBI

By Margot York

Okay, friends. This is serious. Buckle up. Are you ready?

Just days before Logan Asher Wyatt's 18th birthday, a spokesperson for the FBI announced that he is currently being sought for questioning. According to *Scandalicious News's* confidential source within the Bureau, it's about a video.

What kind of video, you ask?

"The kind that gets you a visit from the Feds," our anonymous source stated. "Not terrorism, murder, or any similarly violent acts."

That leaves only one possibility: sex.

What kind of sex?

The kind that gets you a visit from the Feds.

WTF did you do, Logan?

This is breaking news — we'll be updating this story 24/7 as it develops. Don't go anywhere!

Twilight was falling in the valley as the plane landed for the second time that day. Inside, the boy grinned lazily at his kidnapper as she removed the blindfold from his eyes.

"Good to see you again, sugar tits," he drawled. "You've put on weight."

With a dour expression on her face, she took him by the arm and gave it a rough yank to pull him to his feet.

"Let's get you changed," she ordered.

The boy resisted for a moment, putting all the weight of his nearly six-foot frame behind him. His grin became wicked as she faltered, then he obligingly sprang to his feet and hopped down from the airplane cabin to the tarmac of the landing strip.

21

He inhaled deeply and gazed around him: at the blue-black walls of the valley, at the town sunk beneath a gloaming mist, at the school whose windows gleamed like warm honey through the failing light of dusk.

"Feels like home," he said. "If I was fucking Amish."

Keeping her hand firmly—painfully—clamped around his upper arm, she led him to the outbuilding at the edge of the little runway. Inside, folded on the wooden table, were a pair of gray wool trousers, a white button-down shirt, black dress socks, a navy blazer, and of course the purple tie slashed with yellow.

"Put them on. They're the same ones you wore last time. I'm sure they still fit."

"But I'm a growing boy," he said, whipping his designer T-shirt over his head without hesitation to expose a broad chest, a respectable six-pack, and a large black tattoo that hugged his left ribs and hadn't been there the last time he stripped in this shed.

"Look all you want, babe," he said, unzipping his seven-hundred-dollar jeans and lowering them slowly, the way the huge-breasted dancers did at the strip club in L.A. where he and his friends had celebrated his eighteenth birthday. "I'm legal as of three days ago."

His abductor shook her head in disgust.

"Jesus Christ, don't you ever wear underwear?"

"I'm a free-baller," he replied, pulling on the gray wool trousers he remembered all too well.

He slipped on the shirt, buttoned it only halfway, and looped the tie around his neck like a scarf. He shoved his feet into the brown leather dress shoes. They were indeed the same ones he'd taken off for the last time, or so he thought, six months ago.

"Socks," she said.

He grabbed them, stuffed them into the pocket of the blazer, and slung it over his shoulder.

"Let's party," he said.

As she'd done twice before, she conducted him from the plane to the school. She was supposed to deliver him to the headmistress, but he wasn't interested in seeing that dried up old bitch just yet. With a cocky smirk, he wrenched his arm out of her grasp, laughed at her exclamation of annoyance, and began to walk in the opposite direction toward the dining hall.

"Get back here!" she barked.

"I'm hungry," he replied. "I told you, I'm a growing boy."

His stride was confident and unhurried. He didn't look back.

"You're going to get in so much trouble, young man!" she called ineffectually after him.

The boy—who was, in fact, technically a young man now—sauntered through the open double doors of the dining hall without hesitation. He paused on the threshold and surveyed the place, a smug smile on his face. Nothing had changed. Same tantalizing aroma of foods from around the world (he had to admit, the food here was excellent even by gourmet restaurant standards). Same cafeteria-style food service line staffed by impassive adults of murky origins. Same round tables (how egalitarian) scattered over the polished wooden floor. Same unshaded floor-to-ceiling windows offering views of the lake to the north and the town to the east.

Same, same, everything the same.

Nothing had changed, except the faces of the students who stood waiting in line with their trays, or sat chatting and eating in cliquish groups around the tables. Half of them he didn't recognize. The other half he certainly did.

As he strolled through the hall, they recognized him, too.

"Goddammit, no! Why are you back?!" a girl, (Russian, he believed) whom he'd fucked more or less consensually before he left, exclaimed in consternation.

"Good to see you, too," he replied.

"Oh shit!" growled a South American boy he'd always suspected was here for sinister political reasons. "That asshole is back."

"Can't keep a good man down," the young man quipped, making for the front of the cafeteria line. He stepped directly into the path of a kid he didn't know, grabbed the fully loaded tray out of his hands, and strutted away with it.

The kid yelled angrily after him in Korean, but he simply adjusted the drape of the blazer over his shoulder and kept walking.

At the far end of the hall was the old table. His table. He marched straight to it, plunked his tray down, and straddled the empty chair that had always been his.

The kids—three boys and a girl—who were seated at the table looked up in surprise.

A sour smile spread across the girl's face.

"Lord Byron. What the hell are you doing here?" she said.

"Jezebel," he replied, savoring every syllable.

The smile vanished.

"Don't call me that. I've told you."

"How quickly he forgets," grinned Hemlock, a sophomore whose heavy French accent gave his origins away. "She gonna slap you if you say it twice. She slap Machiavelli already three times this week."

Machiavelli, a junior from Nigeria (Lord Byron liked to call him "the Nigerian prince," which enraged him for some reason), shook his head.

"Fuck me, what did you do now? I wish you could tell us."

"And I wish I could tell you," Lord Byron said, winking at him. "It would curl your toes."

"Sex scandal. Has to be," said Saint Augustine, a Swedish boy who was in the same grade as Machiavelli. "Maybe an animal."

The four of them laughed.

His old crew. How he'd missed them.

Jezebel—Jez to everyone except the teachers and the headmistress, lest you feel the fury of her hand upon your cheek—ran her gaze up and down his body appreciatively. She was a senior, like him. Amoral, like him. And insanely devoted to Jesus, unlike him. It kept things spicy between them.

"You're looking sinful, as always," she said in that drowsy, vaguely Southern accent of hers that drove him crazy.

"You too," he said.

He chucked her under the chin like a dirty uncle and dove into the food on his stolen tray: a steaming bowl of bibimbap, a pile of potato-stuffed piroshki, and a handful of chilled crab claws. Just like every kid upon their arrival at the school, he was starving. Their captors didn't provide food during the hours or days spent in transit to wherever the hell this place was. As he wolfed down his dinner, he scanned the dining hall.

"Tell me," he mumbled through a mouthful of hot rice and vegetables. "What've I missed?"

"Da Vinci left," Machiavelli said.

"Cedar left," Jez said.

"Got three new boys. They all left," said Saint Augustine.

"Amethyst and Garnet decided they are lesbians for each other. They won't let you watch, don't even bother asking," said Hemlock. "Stuck-up bitches."

"Don't tell me what to do, son," Lord Byron replied. "What else?"

"Electra's still here," Jez replied. "She'll be…*thrilled* to see you."

"Which one's she?"

"Ukrainian gangster girl. You two screwed in the library the day before you left."

Lord Byron grinned.

"That's who that was," he said. "She certainly did seem thrilled to see me."

"Mr. Cassowary closed the pool for three weeks. I don't know why," said Hemlock. "He make us do jogging in the rain instead. I hate him now."

Lord Byron shoved a piroshki into his mouth whole and bit down, wincing at the way it burned the roof of his mouth. As he chewed, his gaze landed on a small figure seated across the room.

A girl.

She was sitting at a small table with that antisocial he-she asshole Poe. As usual, Poe was ignoring her and everyone around them. The girl was eating just as ravenously as he was.

A new girl.

A sly smile spread across his lips as he swallowed.

New and sexy. Very sexy. Not too young. Seventeen, maybe eighteen, like him. Decent face. Excellent tits.

He pointed his fork at her and gave Jez a nod.

"Who's that?"

Jez turned to look.

"I don't know her name. She got in a couple hours ago."

"Senior?" he asked.

"Junior," she said.

"Her name's Beryl. She's in my L&L class," said Saint

Augustine.

Lord Byron studied her, his smile morphing from sly to lascivious.

"Beryl, huh? My bed. Tonight. First in line," he said. "After you, of course, Jezzie-baby."

Jez rolled her eyes.

"I hear she only likes older men," she replied.

"I heard from Cypress, who heard from Monet, who eavesdropped when she met with Headmistress, that she's here for a sex thing," Machiavelli said, widening his eyes to indicate it had to be true.

Lord Byron grinned in delight.

"Victim or perp?" he inquired.

"Both," Machiavelli replied in an awestruck whisper. "Monet said she got caught on a sex tape banging the president of the United States!"

Jez, the only other American in Lord Byron's crew, snorted.

"No, she didn't. It was just some congressman or something. Here's what I heard," she said, leaning closer to her friends, who followed suit. "I heard the reason she's here is because *Scandalicious News* got ahold of the tape."

Lord Byron's smile vanished. He hated *Scandalicious News* more than anything in the world. If it wasn't for them, he wouldn't be here for the third time. Sick gossip-spreading paparazzi motherfuckers.

"Anyway, the governor or whatever sent her here. Not her family. She's poor," Jez concluded, and the expression on her face indicated that this detail was the most shocking of them all.

Lord Byron cracked a crab claw and regarded the new girl more critically. It must be true; she didn't look rich. Her teeth were neither blindingly white nor uncanny valley straight. No nose job. Definitely no boob job. She wore her uniform stiffly, uncomfortably, as if she'd never worn fine wool in her life. Her tie was knotted so sloppily it was clear she'd never set foot inside a prep school.

He sucked on the crab claw and smirked. Poor girls were infinitely easier than rich girls to seduce.

Across the dining hall, the new girl seemed to feel his gaze. She looked up from her plate and met his eyes. He grinned salaciously at her. She stared back at him for a long moment, then lowered her eyes and continued eating, albeit with less avidity.

Lord Byron set the claw down and pushed his chair back.

"I think I'm going to go on over and welcome—"

But then, a nerve-rattling sequence of three notes, which buzzed as if generated by a twentieth-century synthesizer, pealed forth through the dining hall.

Low note…high note…painfully piercing note like the shriek of a bird of prey.

Everyone instantly fell silent. Every head swiveled to the intercom mounted above the dining hall doors. Even the teachers supervising the meal became motionless and stared fixedly at the speaker.

"Lord Byron," the headmistress's voice boomed, harsh and ominous. "Report to the headmistress's office immediately."

The intercom crackled, then clicked off. Relief relaxed the shoulders of the students and teachers. Lord Byron just sighed.

"Well, I guess we'll have to pick this up later," he said, imitating his father on a business call. "Ladies. And Jez."

"Let's go, Lord Byron," the gym teacher, Mr. Cassowary, called out from across the room.

"Two for the road," Lord Byron said, snatching a pair of lavender macarons from Hemlock's plate.

"Hé! Je te déteste, connard!" Hemlock exclaimed as Lord Byron gave him a flippant salute and sedately backed away from the table.

"Move it," Mr. Cassowary barked, a note of annoyance creeping into his voice.

Lord Byron bit into a macaron and swaggered through the large room, weaving between the tables. As he passed the new girl, he paused. Slowly, he licked his sugar-sticky fingers, one by one. She stared at him, her expression blank.

Cautiously blank. Poor-person blank.

Poe, for their part, scowled at him.

He strolled out of the dining hall, down the corridor leading to the west wing, and up the staircase to the third floor. He ate the second macaron as he strutted down the hall to the familiar office in which he'd spent so much time during his past two sojourns at the school. He wiped his fingers negligently on the seat of his trousers, slipped on the blazer (his only concession to proper decorum), and did a fancy tippity-tap-tap knock on the door, which he knew would annoy the headmistress.

He opened the door and entered before she could say "come in."

He made straight for the chair before her deck, plopped down on it, and stretched his legs out in front of him, his ankles casually crossed.

The headmistress said nothing. Nor did she look at him. Her head was bent over the paper-cluttered surface of her desk. Her right hand held a fountain pen. As her left hand turned over sheets of paper in an absurdly thick manila folder, she made notes on a legal pad.

Lord Byron watched her, mildly amused. When he was younger, this sort of ominous silence from her would have unnerved him.

"Where are your socks?" she inquired at last, not looking up.

"Socks are for gays," he replied with a laugh.

"Put them on," she said.

He gave her a good-natured shrug, kicked off his shoes, and tugged on the socks.

"Happy?" he said. "I live to please."

She lifted her head at last. The expression on her face was dire.

"I hoped to never hear your voice again once your second stay came to an end," she said. "And yet, I'm hearing it now."

He spread his arms wide.

"I'm a bad penny," he said, another of his father's favorite phrases. "I always turn up."

She set the pen down and paged through the file. With deadly deliberation, she withdrew a sheet of paper, held it up, and read it silently. She raised her eyes and regarded him over its upper edge.

"Age fourteen: enrolled following juvenile grand theft auto and involuntary manslaughter convictions. Age sixteen: re-enrolled following out-of-state drug possession, trespassing, and vandalism charges. Age eighteen: re-enrolled. You lasted barely twenty-six weeks before causing another scandal."

"They call that six months on the Outside," he replied. "Six months is a long time. It's practically a—"

"Quiet," she commanded. Even though he was used to her, even though he'd been hardened by countless censure sessions like this one, his breath caught in his chest and his heart skipped a beat.

She closed the file and folded her hands on top of it. She stared at him. He stared back, smiling. It was hard to do. He wanted to look away. But he forced himself not to.

"Do you have anything to say for yourself?"

He pursed his lips, as if pondering his response.

"Yes. For once, it's not my scandal. If you can believe it, I'm not the perp this time. I'm the victim."

Her lips contorted in disgust.

"You've never been a victim in your life."

"I'm just a high-spirited, misguided boy," he replied. This was his mother's pet phrase.

"Is that so?" the headmistress said.

She stared at him. This time, he couldn't maintain his defiant smile, his indifferent gaze. He had to look away, which infuriated him.

"It's no big deal," he said, the defensiveness in his voice audible even to him. "I'm here as a…favor."

"A favor?"

"Yeah, a favor. A very lucrative favor for someone who can do something big for me in return."

A smile—a real one—spread across her face.

"Oh, indeed? How strategic of you. I never pegged you for a gambler, Lord Byron."

He opened his mouth to reply, but she cut him off by standing, pushing her chair in, and walking briskly to the door. To his surprise, she opened it.

She looked at him expectantly.

He hesitated, then rose.

"That's it?" he said.

"That's it," she said lightly. He hesitated again, then shoved his feet into his shoes and made for the door. He stepped through it, hesitated for a third time, and glanced over his shoulder at her.

Her face was wreathed in mirth.

Dreadful, malevolent mirth.

"I'm curious how this gamble will turn out for you," she said. "You know what they say, 'Show me a gambler and I'll show you a loser.' It will be entertaining to watch you lose for the first time in your life."

Chapter 3

It was dark by the time dinner ended. The windows of the dining hall were black and reflective, like enormous pools of still water. Beryl and Poe carried their trays to the dirty rack at the end of the food service line. The big room was deserted; they were the last ones to leave.

"Now what?" Beryl inquired.

"Seven o'clock to eight-thirty, recreation. Eight-thirty to nine, prepare for bed. That includes a shower if you don't like to do it in the morning. Nine-thirty, lights out," Poe stated.

"No phones, no internet," Beryl commented as the two of them exited the dining hall. "What do you guys do for 'recreation' around here? Watch TV?"

"No TV," Poe said, guiding Beryl down the empty hall.

"No TV? Are you kidding?"

"No TV, just movies. But they're all really old. Headmistress only allows VHS tapes."

Beryl let out a dry laugh.

"Wow. It's like living in a renaissance faire."

Poe gave her a flat look.

"I don't know what that is," they said. "And before you ask, there's no radio, either. Nothing broadcast."

Beryl stopped walking.

"That's insane," she said.

"It's to protect us," Poe replied, and they pointedly kept walking. After a moment, Beryl followed.

As the two passed a pair of thick wooden doors that stood wide open, Poe pointed and continued, "After dinner, some people hang out in there. That's the library. It's two stories. Lots of books. It's pretty boring, though. There's nothing from after the 1990s."

"What? Why?"

"To protect us."

"Protect us from what?" Beryl asked, her voice rising in astonishment at the absurdity of it all.

"From someone on the Outside sneaking a message in. All the books and movies and music and stuff are vintage. Printed or recorded so long ago and with such outdated, y'know, materials that nobody Outside could make a fake and sneak it in. Absolutely nothing's digital. We only have VHS tapes for videos, cassette tapes and vinyl records for music, and old books from the twentieth century. Headmistress can tell if they're fakes. Plus she doesn't bring in new stuff very often. If you wreck anything, the other kids'll get really mad at you. Especially if it's one of the tapes. They never get replaced."

Beryl shook her head in amazement as Poe pushed a door open that led to the outdoors.

"Let's cut through the commons. It's faster."

"Where are we going?" Beryl asked as they stepped out into the cool darkness.

"The lounge. All of the kids'll be there."

"Why?"

"Because it's Thursday," Poe said, as if it were obvious.

"Why would th—" Beryl began.

"You ask too many questions," Poe said.

Beryl sighed and clamped her mouth shut as they walked across the vast lawn that lay between the three wings of the building. Silently she mapped the layout of the school in her mind. It was shaped like a square, minus one side. In the middle was the commons—a golf-course-worthy lawn on which a scattering of younger kids were chasing each other and throwing a rugby ball back and forth. At the top of the square was the north wing, where the dining hall and library were. On the left side was the west wing, site of the classrooms and the headmistress's office. At the bottom was the south wing, home to the dorm room she'd be sharing with this unfriendly new buddy of hers. Apparently, it was also the location of the lounge, since it was toward the south wing that Poe was resolutely marching. There was no right side to the square; no east wing. Just the surrounding brick wall, a forbidding iron gate, and a road that led toward the little town that was lost now in the darkness.

"There's a performance hall in the north wing, above the dining hall," Poe said, as if reading Beryl's thoughts. "I don't want to do a tour since it's Thursday, so I'll just tell you. Performance hall, library, dining hall: that's the north wing. Over there: classrooms, gym and pool," they said, pointing at the west wing. "Up ahead, the dorm, student lounge, rec room, and media room for watching movies. There's a small library, too, but it only has encyclopedias and dictionaries and stuff for doing homework. There are a bunch of little study rooms on both floors of the dorm between the bedrooms. They're open to everyone, but some kids act like they belong to them. Especially the girls in the God Squad."

"It seems like a lot of space for just fifty-three students," Beryl observed, picking her way carefully over the grass, which was damp with evening dew. She shivered. An autumnal chill had filled the valley. It was peculiar...it hadn't been autumn when she was kidnapped.

"Fifty-four," Poe corrected. "Another student arrived after you."

"So, we watch old movies and listen to old music and study. That about it?"

Poe stopped walking and looked at her incredulously.

"No," they said. "Don't be stupid. Everybody'd die of boredom. This isn't a reform school, you know. There's tons of activities and a whole bunch of clubs—arts and crafts, theater club, book and music groups, language clubs, all sorts of things. Basically, there's a club or activity for every student's interest since the kids here may be, y'know, *scandalous*, but their parents don't want them to fall behind their peers while they hide out."

"Are all the kids at the school rich?" Beryl asked.

Poe shrugged.

"I guess so."

"How much does it cost to send a kid here?"

"If you have to ask," Poe said. "You can't afford it. Most of us do a sport, too. Horseback riding, swimming, rugby, cricket, soccer. Some boys tried to organize polo teams once, but too many of them got hurt and Headmistress banned it. Dances are a big thing. The God Squad keeps pushing everyone off the organizing committee, though."

"What's the God Squad?" Beryl inquired.

Poe rolled their eyes—but not at Beryl's ignorance, she could tell—and continued walking.

"You'll find out," they said dryly. "They're one of the private clubs. There are a bunch of those. Secret societies. I don't know how they survive. Kids come and go so often."

"How long have you been here?" Beryl asked.

"A long time," Poe replied.

"How long?" Beryl persisted.

"Longer than anyone else."

"Why haven't you left yet?"

"You really ask too many questions," Poe said.

They paused outside the door leading to the south wing.

"One other thing. You should know there are also compulsory clubs."

"Compulsory?"

"To support cover stories. Every kid has a cover story for when they get out. You can't just vanish for weeks and weeks and then roll back into your life like nothing happened. People ask questions. The press asks questions. So your family tells people you were studying abroad in France, or volunteering with a home-building program in Guatemala, or whatever. That means you have to join the French club and learn French and all about French culture, or join the woodworking club and get really good with hammers and saws. It sucks. Kids hate their compulsory clubs. What's your cover story?"

"I—I don't have one," Beryl stammered.

"Well, you'd better think of one," Poe said, opening the door to the lounge. "If you can't come up with something on your own, the headmistress will assign you one. And you probably won't like it. Not one bit."

The student lounge was enormous and so sumptuous Beryl's breath caught in her throat as she entered. A grand piano stood beneath a heavy crystal chandelier. A fire crackled in a massive fireplace whose marble mantle was covered with exotic seashells, heavy brass candelabras, and delicate statuettes. The furniture looked like it had been raided from a magnificent French château, a lavish Indian palace, and the summer residence of a Chinese emperor, yet there was an elegant cohesion to the disparate pieces. Ornate card tables stocked with hand-painted decks and chips that looked as if they were made of real ivory were scattered throughout the space, but nobody was playing. Nobody was doing anything, except waiting.

The room was packed with students who stood around in small groups. Though the place was a lounge, there was nothing relaxed about their demeanors. They murmured to one another without interest. Their tense stances radiated anticipation and impatience. Each of them was entirely focused on the door. When Poe and Beryl entered, they straightened and quieted, then slouched in obvious disappointment and went back to their half-hearted conversations.

"What's going on?" Beryl whispered to Poe as they sidled into the crowded room and worked their way close to the fire to warm up.

"They're waiting for it to get here."

"Waiting for what to get here?"

Just then, a figure appeared in the doorway. A boy. In his arms he carried a tall stack of folded papers that reached to his chin.

"Extra, extra!" he proclaimed in a heavy Korean accent.

Instantly the students came to life. As one, they sprang at him, surrounded him, and grabbed for the papers. Clutching their prizes, the kids retreated to the couches, divans, and window seats. In silence they unfolded the loose pages and began to study them with an intense focus that made Beryl's mouth drop.

"What the hell is going on?" she blurted out.

"Shh!" Poe hissed, their nose buried in their own copy of the mysterious document. Beryl craned her neck to see what it was.

It was a newspaper.

"Want one?" the boy asked, holding out the lone remaining copy, which was bedraggled and torn by grasping hands.

"Sure…" Beryl said, accepting it uncertainly. She glanced at it, then at Poe.

Poe was seated cross-legged on the rug in front of the fire. Beryl moved to sit beside them, then changed her mind. She drifted to a deserted corner of the room, settled onto a plush window seat, and unfolded the newspaper.

The masthead read *School Newspaper.*

There were four headlines on the front page:

"Monday Night Soccer Game Ends in Dramatic Tie"

"Games Committee Announces Poker Tournament Schedule"

"Which Horse is the School's Fastest?"

"Next Week's Lunch Menu"

It was printed on real newsprint. There were no photographs. The bylines above the articles were single names: Electra, Thoreau, Charlemagne, and Shōnagon. Beryl searched each page, but neither the name of a town nor a country were referenced anywhere. There was also no date.

She skimmed the content. It was a typical high school newspaper. And yet, the kids were eating it up. Every one of them was reading the thing like their lives depended on it. Not with apprehension, however. Some grinned, others shook their heads in surprise, still others leaned over to whisper excitedly to a neighbor, pointing at a line of text that caught their eye.

"Who ever heard of a school newspaper being so popular?" Beryl murmured to herself, shaking her head.

"It's the only news we get around here," said a voice behind her, making her jump.

The girl attached to the voice laughed as Beryl raised her head to look at her.

"Sorry," she said. "Mind if I sit here? Garnet keeps elbowing me on the couch."

"Sure," Beryl replied. She scooted over to make room for the girl, who perched on the edge of the narrow seat and paged through her copy of the newspaper until she found a column headlined "Comings and Goings."

"You're going to be here next week. It's a list of students who've arrived and ones who've left," the girl said, pointing at the newspaper proudly. "I write this column."

"You do?"

"Yep. I'm in the newspaper club. It's really fun. We write all the articles, then it gets printed up each week. There's an old-fashioned printing press in the basement under the gym. Charlemagne over there is the typesetter, ever since da Vinci left," she said, indicating the boy who had brought the papers.

"There's a basement in this place?" Beryl said.

"Sure," the girl grinned. "There are all kinds of secret corridors and mysterious rooms. You'd be surprised."

Beryl studied the girl curiously. She was Black and her English was flawless, but her accent wasn't American or British or Australian. Beryl had never been good at identifying accents; it might have been South African or Haitian, or possibly Brazilian Portuguese. She knew better than to ask the girl where she was from, however.

"Newspaper club's the best club," the girl continued. "That's because Mr. Lark runs it. He's everybody's favorite teacher. He's really nice."

Beryl's entire body went numb.

Mr. Lark. Oh God.

Why was he here?

How was he here?

He'd arrived at her high school with a reputation and a name that wasn't "Lark." All the kids steered clear of him. Except her. She was drawn to him.

"I don't care who knows," she'd told him so many times. So many times when they were wrapped in each other's arms. So many times when their naked bodies were pressed close in the velvet darkness. So many times when he told her he loved her but they had to keep this thing of theirs a secret.

"I don't care who knows…"

As it turned out, he was right. When their secret was exposed, everything fell apart. Disastrously.

"I'm Shōnagon, by the way," the girl said. "Isn't that a cool name? Mr. Lark says I'm named after this incredible writer from Japan. She was super famous and really smart."

"I'm named after a rock," Beryl replied.

Her new friend laughed.

"A really expensive rock," Shōnagon said. "Emeralds are a type of beryl stone."

"Oh," Beryl said. "Wow."

"Listen…" Shōnagon glanced around the room and leaned closer to her, lowering her voice confidentially. "I need to warn you.

Don't hang around too much with Poe."

"Why not?" Beryl asked.

"They're a snitch," she whispered. "They tell the headmistress everything. And I mean *everything*."

Beryl raised her head and turned toward the fireplace. Poe was still seated cross-legged on the hearth rug, their newspaper lying discarded next to them. They were frowning at everyone and no one in particular, their chin resting on their balled fist.

"Also," Shōnagon said, jerking her chin at a young man who was striding into the room. "Stay away from that guy."

Beryl shifted her gaze from Poe to the newcomer. It was the boy who'd leered at her in the dining hall. As she watched, he swaggered up to a group of girls, put his arm around one of them, and began to adroitly hit on all of them at once.

"Who is he?" she asked, amazed in spite of herself.

"Lord Byron," Shōnagon said. "Repeat offender."

"Lord Byron?" Beryl repeated. "Seriously?"

Shōnagon nodded.

"It suits him," her new friend said.

"'Mad, bad and dangerous to know,'" Beryl quoted.

"What?" said Shōnagon.

"Nothing..."

He was looking at her. Impudently. Shamelessly. Beryl lowered her gaze for a moment, then raised her eyes and looked back at him.

He smirked knowingly. As if someone had told him all her secrets.

Then he started to walk toward her.

There she was. His next conquest.

He abandoned Jez and the pious pussy patrol without a backwards glance and made his way swiftly through the crowd. He dodged a cluster of Asian kids, elbowed a pair of freshmen aside, and inserted himself between the new girl and the bitch journalist.

"Clear out," he hissed at Shōnagon. She sneered at him and

retreated to a knot of newspaper nerds by the piano, stage-whispering "Remember what I told you!" to the new girl as she departed.

He rearranged his features into the charming, alluring expression he'd perfected: tried and true, it worked on every female from the age of fourteen to forty. Any older and they tended to laugh at him, call him "cutie," and try to set him up with their queer sons for some reason. But this girl was just the right age. Seventeen. Ripe and ready.

"Hey. New girl," he drawled, leaning an elbow against the wall and smiling down at her. "Pleased to meet you. I'm—"

"I know who you are," she said, smiling up at him from the window seat.

It wasn't a nervous smile. Nor was it a shy smile.

It was an intrigued smile.

She was flirting with him. His smile widened with pleasure.

"I know who you are, too," he replied. "You're Beryl."

"I guess," she said. "I just heard that I'm an expensive gemstone."

He liked where this was going.

"Oh, are you?" he said, angling his body closer to hers.

"That's not all I heard," she said.

"Tell me," he said, reaching out to brush a stray lock of hair from her shoulder. She didn't push his hand away.

"I heard…" she lowered her voice. "That I should stay away from you."

"Is that right? Well, I heard…" he leaned down, let his lower lip graze her earlobe, and whispered, "That you like older men."

She recoiled as if his mouth had stung her. Internally he faltered for a moment, though his smile didn't.

"I'm an older man," he continued. "Just turned eighteen. This is your lucky night."

She stared at him.

"Please leave me alone," she said. Her voice was cold.

"Aw, don't be like that," he coaxed, reaching for her hair again. "I'm—"

She grabbed his hand and pushed it away. Hard.

"Leave me alone," she repeated.

He could feel his brow contract in irritation. He forced it to flatten, forced the suave smile to remain in place.

"You got it, baby," he said. "But I'll be back."

As he stepped away, dignity intact, he caught sight of Poe seated on the floor a few feet away. The little shit was eavesdropping. They'd heard everything.

Poe's eyes narrowed. Lord Byron contorted his upper lip into a snarl in response and withdrew to the ever-welcoming embrace of Jezebel.

"Get off me," she ordered, as he draped his arm around her once again. "I thought you'd be on your way upstairs with your new pet by now."

"All in good time," he replied, flicking the tip of his tongue lightly against the side of her neck where her pulse beat strong and steady. She always liked that.

"Strike out," Jez said.

"Strike one," he corrected. "My bat's just getting hard."

"Too bad it's so small," she retorted.

"Okay, people," Mr. Lark announced from the doorway. "Rec time's over."

A collective groan went up.

"Ten more minutes?" one of the kids pleaded.

"I already gave you ten minutes," he replied. "It's nine-ten. Everybody off to bed. Let's go."

He stopped short.

"Lord Byron?" he said in surprise. "I didn't know you were back."

Lord Byron cut his gaze to Beryl to see if she was watching. She was. He gave Mr. Lark a brash grin.

"You know me: I'm incorrigible," he said, his eyes still on Beryl.

"'Mad, bad and dangerous to know,'" Mr. Lark quoted.

Beryl flinched.

Surprised, Lord Byron glanced from her to Mr. Lark.

He was staring at her.

The two of them were staring at each other.

Then quickly—too quickly—they both looked away.

"Bedtime, people. Move it," Mr. Lark commanded, but there was an uncertain quaver in his voice now.

How strange.

Lord Byron ran his tongue over his teeth, musing, as the kids began to file reluctantly out of the lounge.

"I've got an unanticipated vacancy," he said to Jezebel. "Wanna keep me warm tonight?"

"Ha," she said, prying his arm off her shoulders. "You and your five best buddies can keep yourself warm."

She waggled her fingers at him and sashayed out of the room.

He shook his head. So much for a friendly welcome back to school. He gave the new girl a parting grin as she slipped past him, then he swaggered to the door. As he exited, he glanced behind him.

Poe was standing right there, their arms folded over their chest, their eyes narrower than ever.

They'd been watching this, too.

Lord Byron scowled.

He had to do something about Poe. It wasn't going to be like last time, or the time before that, getting ratted out to the headmistress week in and week out. He'd find a way to shake off that spying asshole for good.

Poe flicked the light switch off, pulled back the covers of their bed, and crawled in. Their new roommate was already tucked in tight under her blankets. The bedside lamp illuminated her face. It was wan and weary.

"Are you going to cry?" Poe inquired.

"No."

"You sure?"

"Yeah."

"Good."

Poe was silent for a moment.

"How come you and Lark were looking at each other funny?"

"Who?"

"Mr. Lark. The L&L teacher."

"We weren't looking at each other."

"Yes, you were."

"Well, we weren't looking at each other funny."

"Yes, you were," Poe insisted, propping themself up on their elbow. "I saw you. In class. And again in the lounge."

Beryl was silent for a long time. At last, reluctantly, she spoke.

"I know him from somewhere."

"Where?" Poe asked, their voice breathy with surprise.

This sort of thing wasn't unheard of. The world of the extremely wealthy was small. Every now and then, two kids who knew each other on the Outside happened to be enrolled at the same time. But it had never happened with a teacher.

Never.

"Where do you know him from?" Poe repeated.

"From…a different school," Beryl said.

"What?!" Poe exclaimed.

"It's nine-thirty," Mr. Lark's voice proclaimed from the hallway. "Lights out, people."

Poe was so astonished they couldn't turn off the lamp.

"What school?" they demanded.

"My old high school," Beryl said. "English class."

Poe simply stared at her. How was this possible?

A light rap on the door made them both flinch.

"Lights out, Poe," Mr. Lark's voice from the hallway was muffled but firm. "Right now."

Poe forced themself to turn off the light.

The room went black.

"Good night," Beryl murmured from the darkness.

Poe didn't answer.

They lay awake for a long time, dumbfounded.

It wasn't possible that Mr. Lark was Beryl's high school teacher on the Outside. It simply wasn't possible.

Unless she was lying.

Who was this new girl?

Chapter 4

The stars were shining like strings of fairy lights draped across the black sky when Lark exited the heavy iron gate and stepped onto the road leading to town. He shivered and shoved his hands into the pockets of his khaki trench coat, another mandatory garment from the teacher's uniform.

It was windless and chilly, the quintessence of a crisp autumn night. But every night was windless and chilly in the valley. The weather never changed. It was perpetually autumn. The only explanation for this phenomenon he'd ever gotten came from one of the farmers, whose fertile fields he was passing, hidden within the dense darkness to the south of the road. The farmer was old. He had lived in the valley longer than anyone. Like the rest of the residents, he had no idea where within the geography of the globe they were, but he was convinced the valley was situated such that it created its own microclimate.

Nobody—not the farmer and certainly not Lark—knew whether it was autumn or spring, winter or summer in the mountains that reared high above or the world that lay beyond.

Lark walked briskly along the road. Though it was so dark he couldn't make out his own feet at the ends of his trousers, he had no trouble following the path. He'd walked it so many times he could do it in his sleep.

The first time he'd made the journey to town it was daylight, and he'd been struck by an overwhelming feeling of delight. The path was the very picture of a scenic country road: the dirt packed firm and smooth, the edges girded with nodding grass and a rainbow of frail wildflowers, the view dominated by charming farmland. Now that he'd walked it countless times in light and dark, he knew that its appeal was not accidental but calculated. It was no different than the town and the school and the valley itself. What appeared to be incidental was intentional, what seemed quaint and guileless was artificial and strategic. Even so, it still delighted him to walk down the road on a night like this. It was the only moment of pure freedom he had.

The mile-and-a-half stroll usually cleared his head. But not tonight. He was deeply troubled.

How could she be here?

When he arrived on the outskirts of town it was a little after ten o'clock. The warm yellow lights of the cottages where he, his fellow teachers, and the townsfolk lived welcomed him. Like the country road leading to the school, the town was uncannily picturesque. Each cottage was surrounded by a white picket fence that enclosed a neatly clipped lawn. Each home sported a generous porch upon which you were encouraged to sit on sunny days and greet passersby in a neighborly manner. We're all friends here: that was the motto of the town, and like the town itself, the sentiment was unnaturally whimsical.

Emerging from the rows and rows of cottages, his footsteps took him onto the main street of the town. It had no name. It needed no name. The grocery store and tailor comprised the street's western side. Its eastern side included a movie theater, a coffee shop where he got a latte every morning before the walk to school, a bookstore with a surprisingly decent (albeit outdated) paperback selection, and a restaurant. All along the street, the old-fashioned iron lamp posts glowed with strings of white lights that rivaled the stars above. Boxes of tulips and nasturtiums, changed daily to maintain their flawless freshness, lined the sidewalk. The street was romantic, enchanting, and synthetic, like the set from a rom-com movie.

The sign above the door of the restaurant read "La Cage Dorée" in hand-painted gold script. He entered, eager to escape the nippy night air. Even at this late hour, the tables were covered with immaculate white tablecloths, with formal place settings and flickering candles in delicate glass globes. One of them was occupied by Frau Grouse, who ran the bookstore. At the other sat Jay.

His best friend.

His only friend, really.

Jay looked up when a gust of brisk air rushed in with Lark. A smile spread across his face.

"Hey Lark," he called out.

"Hey Jaybird," Lark responded, shrugging out of his coat and hanging it on the brass rack by the door. "Did you order?"

"Yep. I'm getting an apple tart. You're getting apple strudel and coffee."

Lark had already eaten dinner in the teacher's dining room at school hours ago. These after-work desserts with Jay were a special indulgence of his, saved for nights when he had bedtime supervision duty.

"Did you personally vet the apples?" he joked as he sat.

Jay nodded seriously.

"The orchard master wanted to hold off the harvest for another week, but I talked him into collecting a bushel of Braeburns that were on the verge of becoming windfall. Long day. I'm beat, man."

Jay worked in logistics. Officially, his title was Administrator of Nutriment Inventory and Procurement. It was his job to keep track of the town's food supply. His bible was an enormous ledger filled with records of what was coming from the farms and orchard, and what was needed from the Outside. The school had its own administrator of nutriment inventory and procurement, and got first dibs on the choicest produce. Still, the farms couldn't provide everything. Someone else—someone Lark didn't know and Jay couldn't talk about—placed orders each week for additional food for the school and town with contacts on the Outside.

His friend frequently longed aloud for a computer. And a truck. There were no vehicles in the valley. The farmers tended their fields with horse-drawn plows and brought their food to town via horse-drawn drays. Jay made daily treks of six miles on foot between the farms at the central and southern end of the valley and the orchard north of the town to forecast the coming weeks' food deliveries and predict potential shortfalls. When Lark questioned the absence of motorized vehicles early in his tenure as a teacher, Jay told him, "Vehicles can neither heal nor reproduce. Horses can. But God, I wish I had a truck!"

"I'm surprised you were free tonight," Jay commented. "I thought you were on overnight duty this week."

"I was," Lark replied. "But Cassowary got re-assigned the overnight this morning. He also had the dining hall shift today. He must have done something to piss off the headmistress."

A waiter noiselessly appeared and placed two plates of dessert and a cup of coffee on the table. Lark dug in. It was excellent. It never ceased to amaze him that there was a world-class restaurant in this remote valley.

Nor did it cease to amaze him that it was free.

Everything in the valley was free. The treats he shared with his friend, the latte he drank every morning, the books in the bookshop, the clothes on his back, the food on the grocery store shelves. Even the cottage and all the utilities that made it comfortable didn't cost him a cent.

There was a trade-off, of course: everything was free, but nobody was paid.

The place was a communist's wet dream.

"So," Jay said, shoveling a mouthful of hot apples and pastry crust into his mouth. "I saw two planes arrive today. Not supply planes. Did we get a couple new kids?"

Jay was intimately aware of the comings and goings of aircraft in the valley. There was no hiding anything from him.

Lark nodded.

"That's pretty unusual, isn't it?" said Jay. "Two in one day?"

Lark nodded again.

"What's really unusual is one of them is a repeat offender," he said. "Guess who's back?"

"Who?" Jay asked.

"Lord Byron."

Jay dropped his fork onto his china plate with a clatter.

"No fucking way!" he exclaimed. "I thought we'd seen the last of that little shit."

"Me too."

Jay shook his head in disgust.

"How is that even possible? Is that kid a scandal machine?"

"I guess so."

"Well..." Jay said, picking his fork back up and giving Lark a wry smile. "You must be overjoyed."

46

Lark took a sip of coffee, wishing it were beer or something stronger. Alcohol was forbidden in the valley. He'd spent more than a few evenings complaining to Jay about Lord Byron and wishing he could drink his aggravation away.

Though he was six years older than the boy, Lord Byron reminded him of his older brother. The cocky smirk. The complete disregard for others. The casual cruelty. The way he always, always got away with it.

Lark hated his older brother more than anyone in the world.

Perhaps to prevent another evening of bitter gripes, Jay said, "Speaking of planes, I had to put in an order for wasabi root and nori sheets today. Our beloved Cage Dorée is going to offer a sushi menu in the next few weeks."

"Sounds tasty. It's been a long time since I had sushi," Lark replied, and he was grateful to Jay for changing the subject before he could ask him about the other student that had arrived today.

As Jay rattled off a litany of exotic fish and condiments that would be arriving in the coming days, Lark stared into his coffee cup, his mind slowly revolving along the same circular path it had traveled since the moment she stepped into his classroom.

How could she be here?

How could she be here?

How could she be here?

He'd never believed in soul mates before he met her.

He'd never felt as close to anyone as he had to her.

He would have done anything for her.

"I'll do anything for you," he'd murmured the night they had sex in yet another secret place, far from prying eyes. The night he sensed she was becoming impatient with him, pulling away from him.

"You know what I want you to do," she'd replied, her voice tense and aloof. "If you really loved me, you'd do it."

But he couldn't—not that, not what she was asking.

He couldn't...until he could. He did it. And everything went terribly, violently wrong.

"Lark? Hey, Lark?"

"Hm?"

"Everything okay?" Jay inquired.

"Sure."

"You're real quiet tonight."

"I'm just tired."

He wished he could tell his friend what was bothering him. But he didn't dare.

"The curfew warning blew, you know."

That got Lark's attention.

"What? When?"

"About fifteen minutes ago. We'd better get going."

"Right, right," Lark said, standing with alacrity and tossing his napkin onto the table. All the candles in the restaurant had been extinguished. The lights in the kitchen were off. Frau Grouse was long gone.

Curfew was signaled with the same trio of eerie notes as the intercom at the school. First the long, low note: a warning that curfew was coming. Twenty minutes later, the high note would ring out. Then, just five short minutes after that, the skin-crawling shriek would sound, lasting for a full minute. A minute was all the time you had to get your ass inside your home where you belonged. Then silence. The silence was more disturbing than the cacophony that preceded it. If you heard it while standing outside your house, it meant you were in violation of curfew.

You did not want to violate curfew.

Absolutely, positively not.

As he and Jay grabbed their coats from the rack by the door, the second siren sounded. The sustained, mournful high note raised the hairs on the back of Lark's neck.

"Five minutes," Jay said, clapping a hand on Lark's shoulder. "Good to see you, man."

"You too," Lark said; he was already half-jogging up the street, making for the cottages.

Jay's apartment was just across the street, above the grocery store. He'd have no trouble making it home in time.

Lark might not.

He hurried down the sidewalk, heading north. Behind him, the Victorian-style lamps on their iron posts began to extinguish, one by one. He picked up his pace. He was practically running now.

From the southern edge of town, he heard a faint grinding sound. He broke into a sprint.

Just ahead, the cottages emerged from the dark, their bright windows beckoning to him, urging him to hurry. He was the only soul still outside.

He heard the grinding sound again and dashed past his neighbor's bungalow. His was just ten yards from home.

The grinding sound was coming closer. His cottage was dead ahead.

He vaulted over his white picket fence, leapt up the steps leading to his porch, and seized the front doorknob.

He wrenched the door open—he had no key, nobody's cottage had a lock, *we're all friends here*—and darted inside. He slammed the door behind him just as the final curfew siren blew. The excruciating screech rang out for sixty seconds as he leaned against the door panting, his heart pounding like a jackhammer.

Then, silence.

He let out a sigh of relief. He kicked off his shoes, loosened his tie, and sank into his living room chair.

Everything was all right now.

Except…it wasn't.

Everything was all wrong. Because she was here.

How could she be here? How how how?

He had a dreadful feeling she was going to get him in trouble. Again.

The look on her face that awful night.

The words, spoken in an urgent whisper, "Do it."

The scandal.

But maybe…

Maybe instead of getting him in trouble, this time he'd get *her* in trouble.

He'd force her to make up for everything he'd been through.

She owed it to him for ruining his life.

Chapter 5

Beryl had just taken her first bite of dinner Friday night when three harsh notes echoed through the dining hall.

Bung…bing…BEEEEE!

All conversation ceased, all heads swiveled, and all eyes zeroed in on the intercom.

"Beryl," it declared. "Come to the headmistress's office in fifteen minutes."

"Uh-oh," proclaimed a jocular voice she didn't recognize after the speaker crackled to silence. "What'd you do?"

Scattered laughter, a resumption of conversation, and Beryl found that she had lost her appetite. She picked at her white truffle risotto, then sighed and stood.

"Might as well get it over with," she said, trying to grin carelessly. "I'll score points for being early, right?"

Poe snorted.

"Good luck with that," they said.

"Come with me?" Beryl said.

"No way," Poe replied. "You know where it is."

Beryl sighed again and carried her tray to the dirty rack.

She'd done her best to fit in. What had she done wrong?

"So," said the headmistress, settling into the wingback chair across from the leather divan on which Beryl was nervously perched. "How do you feel your first full day of school went?"

"It was fine," Beryl replied.

The headmistress cocked her head.

"Fine? Are you sure?"

"It was okay," Beryl said.

The headmistress said nothing. She simply smiled inscrutably at Beryl.

Beryl began squirm.

The headmistress continued to smile.

"It was hard," Beryl admitted.

The headmistress's smile widened. It became almost (but not quite) indulgent, almost (but definitely not) warm.

"Thank you for being transparent with me," she said.

Beryl let out a ragged sigh.

"I don't think my old school was very good," she said. "I worked hard, I got good grades, but I feel like an idiot here."

She hadn't just felt like an idiot today. She'd looked like one, too.

The school day started at nine o'clock and consisted of five classes, an hour each, plus an hour for lunch. Poe had pointed her in the direction of each classroom, ever more resentfully as the day wore on. The classes were small, just a dozen or fewer students in each. That made it impossible to simply sit quietly and try to get her bearings.

In history and geography, she failed to correctly identify both the dates of the Liberian civil war and the location of the country itself on a map, much to the entire class's amusement and the teacher's disgust.

In science, she'd been incapable of answering a single question when the teacher grilled her on her knowledge of kinetic energy, torque, and angular impulse. She'd stood there in front of the rest of the students, open-mouthed, unable to fathom what any of it had to do with mitosis and the nitrogen cycle, until she realized the class was physics, not biology.

In math class, she stared in bewildered dismay at a tangle of derivative, limit and integral symbols, her pencil standing rigid between her fingers, until class ended. "It's just calculus, not algebraic topology," the teacher said impatiently when she handed in her quiz completely blank. "A girl your age should have no trouble with this."

In gym, the teacher berated her when she lagged behind the other kids during a dreary jog from the riding grounds to the soccer field. "I know thirty-year-olds who've got more stamina than you, Beryl!"

Only in the final class of the day, language and literature, had she felt slightly comfortable—but only slightly, because the sight of Mr. Lark unnerved her to the point of panic. He seemed as uneasy with her presence as she was with his. To her relief, he sent her to the writing lab to attempt an essay on a poem the class had read and discussed yesterday.

"Do your best," he said, handing her a musty old book with the text bookmarked, his hand not entirely steady. "I'm an easy grader. Isn't that right, people?"

At this, the class groaned in denial.

"You can go type it up when you're ready," he added as she returned to her seat to read the poem. She scanned the text and the words struck her as disconcertingly familiar.

Like a poet hidden in the light of thought, singing hymns unbidden, till the world is wrought to sympathy with hopes and fears it heeded not...

He had read these verses aloud to her one night after they'd made love.

She sat staring at the poem, the letters blurring to form a nonsensical jumble, for a quarter of an hour while Mr. Lark's voice rose and fell in a lecture about the Lake Poets. Then she shook herself and willed her mind to concentrate on coming up with a thesis and theme. When she had them, she rose, exited the classroom, and walked down the hall to the writing lab.

The place was empty, to her relief. But to her shock, there wasn't a computer in sight. Instead, on each of the desks stood a clunky manual typewriter.

She had never used—or even seen—a real typewriter in her life. She sat down at a desk behind one of the bulky machines and stared at it for a long time. Then, hopelessly, she began twisting knobs and whacking levers and banging keys, striving to force prose from the recalcitrant thing.

She trudged back to L&L forty minutes later, handed Mr. Lark two smudged and typo-riddled sheets of paper, and sank into her seat just as class—and the school day—ended at three o'clock.

While the other kids headed for the study rooms and library to tackle their homework, she'd returned to her dorm room and fell face-down on her bed. She felt exhausted and stupid.

"I think Monday will be better," Beryl concluded without optimism.

The headmistress leaned back in her chair and crossed her legs. She was wearing a cherry-red blazer with decorative gold chains on the pockets and enormous shoulder pads today, along with a matching skirt and nylons a shade darker than her skin tone. She looked like a newscaster from the 1980s.

"What do you think of your roommate?" she inquired.

"They're nice. Nice enough," Beryl amended, before the headmistress could give her the inscrutable look again.

"Most children find Poe difficult to get along with."

"We're getting along okay."

"Mmm," the headmistress replied, and Beryl didn't like the knowing look she gave her.

"So, where are we? What country?" Beryl asked. "I think you were going to tell me yesterday."

"I know I wasn't going to tell you anything of the sort," the headmistress replied with a laugh. "You're safely hidden. That's all you need to know."

"How many students are here?"

"Fifty-four," the headmistress replied, "I believe you asked that yesterday as well."

"It just seems like this place is way too big for fifty-four students."

"Does it?"

"Did this used to be something else? Like a sanatorium or something?"

"Sanatorium," the headmistress marveled. "That's quite a big word for such a little girl."

Beryl's cheeks reddened.

"I'm not a little girl. And I read a lot."

"I see. Does this look like a former sanatorium to you?"

"I don't know," Beryl said. "I've never seen one before."

"Then I ask you: if you've never seen one before, of what use would knowing whether this was once a sanatorium be to you?"

"I..." Beryl could feel the color in her cheeks deepen. "I don't know."

The headmistress regarded her. Her lips pursed in a shrewd moue.

"You're a very inquisitive girl," she said at last. "Let me give you a piece of advice."

She leaned closer to Beryl and gestured at her to do the same.

"Suppress it," she said.

"Suppress what?" Beryl asked uneasily.

"Your inquisitive nature. It will only make your stay here a very..." she paused, and the look in her eyes became undeniably sinister. "A very unhappy one."

When Beryl emerged from the headmistress's office, the west wing was deserted. She trekked back to the north wing, expecting to find a small crowd in the library or a few stragglers in the dining hall, but both were empty. She poked her head into the performance hall, but it was dark and silent.

So much for the vibrant social life Poe had promised. Then again, it was Friday night. Maybe all the action was in the dorms. She exited the north wing, trotted across the commons, and entered the lounge on the ground floor of the south wing, shivering from the biting evening air.

A cheery fire crackled in the fireplace, the card tables stood waiting, the window seats and couches offered a cushy invitation, but not a soul was in the place.

Where was everyone?

"There you are!"

She jumped and whirled around.

In the doorway stood Shōnagon.

"I've been looking for you," she said. "Do you want to get ready together?"

"Get ready for what?" Beryl asked.

"The dance. Every Friday there's a dance."

"I don't know," Beryl said. "I'm kind of tired."

Shōnagon laughed and grabbed her hand.

"You sound like an old woman," she said. "Come on."

The girl tugged Beryl out of the lounge, up the stairs to the second floor, and down the hall before she could utter a word of protest.

"Let's get your dress first," Shōnagon said, opening the door to the room Beryl shared with Poe without knocking. Beryl expected an irritable admonishment to greet them, but her roommate was nowhere to be seen. "We'll get ready in my room. I've got a ton of hair stuff. My old roommate left it behind when she left."

"I wonder where Poe is," Beryl said, as Shōnagon yanked her closet door open and began rifling through her clothes.

"They're on the dance organizing committee, so they're down in the gym with the God Squad getting things ready. Poe's the only person those bitches haven't been able to run off."

Shōnagon pulled a black garment bag that Beryl hadn't noticed from the very back of the closet.

"Here we go," she said.

"What's that?" Beryl asked.

"You'll see," Shōnagon replied. "Let's go."

As they hustled down the hall to Shōnagon's room, Beryl noted that all the other doors were closed. Muffled bursts of conversation and laughter leaked out into the hallway.

"What else do kids do for fun on Friday nights?" she asked as Shōnagon opened the door to her room.

Shōnagon gave her a puzzled look.

"What do you mean?" she said. "I told you. Friday night is dance night."

"Ah," Beryl said. "It's mandatory."

"No way," Shōnagon said, ushering her inside. "Dances are great. Nobody ever misses them. Unless they're really, really sick or something."

Shōnagon's room was indistinguishable from Beryl's: a cozy chambre de bonne bedroom with a low ceiling and two narrow beds situated opposite each other, separated by a window and a nightstand. An early nineteenth-century wardrobe and dresser stood at the foot of each bed. The wooden floor was worn to an even, grainless texture, its dark surface half-hidden by the same dull red Turkish rug that covered Beryl's floor. Across one bed lay a garment bag just like the one Shōnagon pulled from Beryl's closet. On the dresser closest to it was a comb and brush, an array of ribbons, and a pile of elastic hair ties. On the nightstand was a huge basket of condoms.

Shōnagon saw her looking at it and grinned.

"Dances aren't the only thing kids do for fun," she said. "Let's get dressed. We're going to be late."

She unzipped Beryl's garment bag and pulled out a dress. Beryl inhaled sharply in surprise.

It was the most beautiful dress she'd ever seen.

The fabric was silver-gray, nearly the same shade as the wool skirt of her uniform, but so delicate and shimmery it looked like it was woven of gossamer. She reached out and tentatively stroked the skirt, which was as soft as a flower petal.

"Is this silk?" she asked.

"Of course. Mulberry silk, the best kind," Shōnagon said, thrusting the dress at Beryl and turning to unzip her own garment bag. She pulled out an identical dress. "It's part of the school uniform. For semi-formal dances."

"This is a semi-formal dress?" Beryl repeated in astonishment.

The gown was more exquisite than any garment she'd seen in her life. It looked like it belonged on the body of a movie star, not draped on a hanger she held in her own hand.

"Yeah," Shōnagon said, unzipping her wool skirt and kicking off her shoes. "The formal gowns are really nice. We have a formal dance every eight weeks. Semi-formals every four. The other dances are casual, sometimes with a fun theme. We had a pajama dance two weeks ago. That was crazy."

Shōnagon shed her tie, blazer and blouse, then unhesitatingly yanked the silken gown over her head as if she were pulling on a grungy old sweatshirt. Beryl blanched. She was too intimidated to do more than clutch her hanger and gawk.

"Zip me up," Shōnagon commanded, pivoting to present her

back to Beryl. Beryl warily grasped the zipper tab, prayed she wouldn't jam or tear anything, and pulled it up.

Shōnagon inspected herself in the full-length mirror on the inside of her wardrobe door. She met Beryl's eyes in the reflective glass.

"Well, go on," she laughed. "It's not going to bite you."

"So this is what it's like to be a rich kid," Beryl murmured.

"What?" said Shōnagon.

"Nothing," she replied.

She took a deep breath and unbuttoned her blouse.

"You're so stiff," Shōnagon commented as they descended the staircase to the ground floor twenty minutes later. "Loosen up, don't you ever wear dresses?"

"Not nice ones," Beryl replied. "I don't feel like I'm wearing it—I feel like it's wearing me."

Shōnagon laughed.

"Well, relax," she said. "It won't spontaneously shred or anything."

Beryl glanced down at herself. The silvery bodice embraced her waist and breasts as though it were in love with her. The cloudlike skirt flared and floated, defying gravity with each step she took. The dress felt alive to her. Even if the gown was wearing her, it felt superb against her skin. It made her feel grand, chic. Like a princess.

When they reached the bottom of the staircase, Shōnagon hesitated for a moment, then put her hand on Beryl's wrist.

"There's something you should know," she said, her tone confidential. "There's a rumor going around about you."

Beryl's jaw clenched. She gripped the railing convulsively.

"What rumor?"

"That you're really…" Shōnagon lowered her voice. "Poor."

Beryl's jaw relaxed and she let go of the railing.

"I guess you could say that," she admitted. "Compared to everybody here, at least."

Shōnagon's dark eyes were sympathetic.

"What's it like?"

"Being poor?"

"Yeah."

"Um..." Beryl let out a chuckle. "I don't know. It felt...normal. Until I came here."

Shōnagon nodded, as if what she'd always suspected were true. Beryl wondered about her background. How rich was she? How sheltered? If the most gorgeous garment Beryl had ever seen was a casual frock to this girl, what sort of lifestyle did she lead on the Outside?

Just ahead, the doors to the gym stood open. Loud music was pouring out.

"How's my hair?" Shōnagon demanded, turning her head from side to side for Beryl's inspection.

"Perfect," Beryl replied.

"Yours looks good, too. I wish they let us have hairspray, though. Ready?"

Beryl nodded, an unexpected wave of nervousness washing over her.

They stepped into the gym.

The harsh overhead lights were all turned off. Glittering disco balls hung from the netball hoops. At each corner of the enormous room stood racks of spotlights covered with colored gels. Sparkling rainbows reflected off the glossy floor. The students were bathed in color, and Beryl was, too. She felt disoriented, as if she were standing within a dark prism.

The kids were dancing with unaffected enthusiasm. The girls all wore the same dress that she and Shōnagon had on. The boys were clad in gray dinner jackets and matching trousers, the bow ties at their necks exactly the same purple with yellow stripes as their regular school ties. Everyone looked elegant, sophisticated, and older than their years. But there was something strange about their appearance. It wasn't that they were teenagers dolled up like millionaires at a gala fundraiser. It was something else.

All at once, she realized what it was.

Their ears, necks, and wrists were all decidedly bare. There wasn't a necklace or wristwatch or ring or earring to be seen.

"Nobody's wearing jewelry," she said.

"Of course not," Shōnagon replied. "Jewelry's forbidden. They take it away from you when you arrive. That's why they watch you strip in that gross shed. I heard that one time, before they started watching, a girl got in with a toe ring. Nobody noticed until it was too late. She got in big trouble, I heard."

"Why is jewelry such a big deal?" Beryl asked.

"It's an identifier," Shōnagon explained. "If you're wearing one-of-a-kind earrings from a famous jeweler, or an heirloom necklace, or some kind of cultural or religious ornament, people might figure out who you are."

"Like who?"

"Other kids. We're our own worst enemies," Shōnagon said. "Weren't you wearing any jewelry when you came here?"

"No," Beryl replied.

When she agreed to be kidnapped, she'd been warned not to wear any jewelry. But she wasn't told why.

Out on the dance floor, an Asian boy jumped up and down, waving his arm.

"Hey, Shōnagon! Wanna dance?" he called out. His name was Charlemagne, Beryl remembered. He brought the newspapers yesterday.

"Sure!" Shōnagon exclaimed, and she vanished into the throng of bodies shuffling and writhing together under the polychromatic lights.

Beryl stood watching for a moment, an odd mixture of bemusement and nostalgia churning within her. She'd gone to a couple of school dances when she was a naive fourteen-year-old, but they were sparsely attended and boring as hell. The kids just stood around staring at their phones, occasionally venturing across the dance floor to talk to someone they knew, then retreating to the shadows.

These kids were actually dancing with each other. Dancing eagerly and energetically to a Flock of Seagulls song, of all things. On a whim, Beryl began counting the couples. Twenty-one. That made forty-two students dancing. Plus herself, plus Poe, who was still nowhere to be seen.

Forty-four students in total.

She frowned.

The headmistress told her there were fifty-four.

Where were the other ten?

She counted the students again.

Forty-four.

As she began a third tally, her eyes drifted to the chaperons, who were standing at the edge of the dance floor, watching the kids and chatting. Mr. Cassowary, the gym teacher, who accused her of having no stamina. Mr. Crane, the history and geography teacher, who probably thought she was a crypto-racist for her ignorance about the geopolitical chronology of the continent of Africa. And...

Oh God...

Mr. Lark.

His face was turned away from her. His profile, so familiar to her heart yet so different to her eyes, was spattered with luminous oranges and yellows. The light picked up the reddish highlights in his brown hair. She felt a pang of longing.

They'd never danced together. What would it be like to feel his arms around her, their bodies swaying slowly together, their lips meeting...

He turned.

Their eyes met.

She stared at him. He stared at her.

He was going to ruin everything for her.

With a start, she forced herself to look away. She ducked her head and retreated blindly, her silken skirt tangling between her legs. She was brought to a painful halt when her hip jolted against a solid surface.

"Watch it," Poe's flat voice barked. "You'll make it spill."

Poe was standing at attention behind a long table draped with an elegant damask tablecloth. At its center stood an enormous crystal punch bowl nearly overflowing with murky orange liquid. Poe held a silver ladle in one hand and an empty punch glass in the other.

"Want some?" they inquired.

"No thanks," Beryl said.

"You can have one glass. One," Poe emphasized. "Once everybody's had a glass, you can have seconds. Not before."

"Okay," Beryl said. "Good to know."

"Why were you looking at Mr. Lark like that?" Poe asked.

Beryl's heart seized. Had she been so obvious?

He wasn't the one who was going to ruin everything: she was doing a pretty good job of it on her own.

"I'm—I wasn't," she stammered. "I was just…counting kids."

"Why?" Poe said.

"I was wondering how many kids are here."

"Everyone's here," Poe replied.

"Really?"

"Of course," Poe said. "Nobody would miss it. Dances are one of the most fun things we get to do."

Her inquisitive nature…she should suppress it. That's what the headmistress told her.

But she couldn't.

"How many students are enrolled in the school?" she asked.

"Forty-four."

"Forty-four? You're sure? Only forty-four?" Beryl repeated.

"Yeah," Poe said with annoyance. "Why do you care?"

Forty-four.

What about the other ten? Had the headmistress lied to her? If so, why?

It made no sense.

"You were flirting with Lord Byron yesterday," Poe said.

"What? No," Beryl protested. "He was just introducing himself."

"You flirted with him," Poe repeated. "That's what he thinks, anyway. You'd better be careful."

"Of what?"

"Of him. He's a bad person."

"Poe!" a sharp voice suddenly shouted.

Beryl turned to see a tall girl with a thick mane of blonde hair marching through the crowd. She wore an angry scowl on her strikingly pretty face. As if Beryl were invisible, she shouldered her aside and came to a halt before the punch bowl.

"How come you told Hecate she couldn't have another glass of punch?"

She had a trace of a Southern accent, Beryl noted, along with an air of command that made her seem far older than a teenager.

"One glass per student," Poe stated. "Once everybody's had a glass, she can have seconds."

The girl folded her arms under her impressive bosom and thrust out her chin belligerently.

"That's stupid. You give me a glass for her," she said, holding out a hand. Her fingernails were very long, unpolished, and completely real.

"After everybody's had one. Not before."

"You aren't the boss of the punch!" the girl barked.

"Not before!" Poe insisted.

Music for a slow dance began to play. With the smoothness of a Ferrari sliding into a parking space, Lord Byron slipped in between the bickering duo and Beryl.

"Hi there," he said.

"Hi," Beryl replied, startled by his abrupt appearance.

He ran his eyes up and down her figure. His gaze lingered on her cleavage. A brazen smile formed on his full lips.

He held out his hand, the palm facing up.

"Dance with me," he said.

Beryl glanced at Poe. They were shaking their head stubbornly at the blonde girl, who had launched into a full-scale jeremiad about Poe's mismanagement of the refreshments.

"Okay," Beryl said uncertainly.

She placed her hand in his. His thumb stroked her knuckles. He gave her a wink.

Something about this felt wrong. Poe's words echoed in her mind: *You'd better be careful of him. He's a bad person.* As he led her toward the crowd of dancers, he glanced over his shoulder. Not at her, but at the blonde girl. The girl flashed him a triumphant smile.

Had they planned this?

Had he asked her to distract Poe so he could maneuver Beryl away?

"Actually," she said, coming to a halt before they could step onto the dance floor. "I don't think I want to."

"Too late," he said, and his grip on her hand tightened. He

pulled her out onto the floor, directly under the shifting, multicolored lights.

"No, seriously," she protested. "I changed my mind—"

He yanked on her arm and her words were transformed into a gasp. She stumbled, falling against his chest. Instantly his hand tightened around hers, while his other arm cinched around her waist like a steel belt.

"Stop it," she said, squirming. "I don't want to dance with you."

Lord Byron began to move his feet in time to the music.

"I know all about you," he murmured, gazing down at her as he forced her to sway along with him. She struggled, but his arms held her firmly against his hard body.

"Let me go," she ordered.

"I know your secret," he said.

She stopped resisting. She stared up at him in horror.

"What do you mean?" she said.

"I know who you are…" he crooned in a singsong voice, lowering his lips to her neck.

She went rigid with fear.

Was it possible?

Did he know?

"You're…" he grazed his teeth against her skin. "A romance girl. You're into sparkly vampires and shit like that."

"Oh, for Christ's sake!" she cried, her body writhing once again against his. "Let go of me. I said, let go of me!"

"Not a chance," he murmured, trying to work a hickey into her flesh.

"Let go of me, Logan!" she shouted.

But he didn't hear her because, at that moment, a hand landed on his shoulder.

It belonged to Mr. Lark.

"Keep it clean," he said. "You know the rules."

"Relax," Lord Byron replied, shrugging off Mr. Lark's hand. "We're all adults here."

Beryl's eyes widened. She opened her mouth to interject, but Mr. Lark spoke first.

"I think you'd better sit this one out," he said.

Lord Byron snorted and turned his back on his teacher, still holding Beryl securely in his embrace.

"I don't think so," he retorted.

Mr. Lark's hand descended upon the boy's shoulder again. Hard.

"You're done. Go to your room," he commanded. "Now."

Lord Byron released Beryl and wheeled on Mr. Lark.

"Are you fucking for real?" he bellowed, his face turning red.

Around them, the students stopped dancing. The music stuttered, then went silent.

"Yes," Mr. Lark replied. "I am fucking for real."

Beryl heard muted gasps.

Lord Byron took a step toward his teacher.

"Make me," he said.

Hot, implacable anger kindled in Mr. Lark's eyes. Beryl's throat clenched with dread. She'd seen this rage once before, on the last night they'd spent together.

Just before the blood began to flow.

"You heard Mr. Lark," Mr. Cassowary's deep voice rumbled. "Need me to say it, too?"

The gym teacher stepped up behind his colleague. He was joined by the history and geography teacher.

Lord Byron glanced at Mr. Cassowary, then at Mr. Crane, then at Mr. Lark. A wintry sneer settled like a mask over his handsome features.

"Nope," he gibed. "I was getting bored with this kiddie bullshit anyway. Let's go, guys."

He snapped his fingers, turned on his heel, and sauntered off the dance floor. Saint Augustine from Beryl's L&L class and two boys she didn't know followed him. As he passed the blonde girl, he jerked his head at her to come along, but she just watched him go, smirking with amusement from the arms of the boy she'd been dancing with. The four boys exited the gym, one of them giving the door a kick as he left.

"Show's over," Mr. Crane announced. "Let's get the music back on, Medusa."

The girl who was playing DJ cued up a very loud Bon Jovi song and the kids began to dance again, first tentatively, then as zealously as before.

Mr. Cassowary and Mr. Crane drifted back to the sidelines. Mr. Lark remained by her side.

"Are you okay?" he asked. It was a perfectly innocent question. Just a teacher checking on his student.

She nodded, glanced around, and bit her lip.

All the kids were dancing. No one was looking at them.

She grabbed the sleeve of his tweed jacket.

"I need to talk to you," she whispered urgently.

"Not here," he whispered back, pulling his arm away. "Give me a few minutes. I'll take us somewhere safe."

He strode away calmly, as if nothing had passed between them.

But something had. Acknowledgment. Confession. Recognition of their guilty past.

Beryl turned away from his retreating form. As her eyes roved the gymnasium, they landed on someone who was not dancing. Someone who was watching her intently.

Poe.

Poe had seen everything.

Beryl swallowed nervously as her roommate's eyes narrowed.

She had a feeling this wouldn't end well.

Not for any of them.

Chapter 6

The last siren for curfew had just sounded. Lord Byron swung the stick angrily, whacking underbrush out of his way, while behind him Saint Augustine, Machiavelli, and Hemlock roughhoused and giggled. Like the stupid kids they were. It took all his self-control not to turn around and smack them.

The entrance to the path that led from the school to the lake was concealed by a dense thicket of evergreen bushes and low-hanging tree branches. Its existence was a secret handed down from student to student. None of the adults at the school knew about it. Not even the headmistress. Lord Byron swung the stick and wished the limbs he struck were Mr. Lark's.

He couldn't believe the man had humiliated him like that. In front of the entire school.

If he knew who Lord Byron's father was, he'd—

"Knock it the hell off!" he shouted, rounding on his friends and striking out with his stick. He landed a solid blow against Machiavelli's shoulder.

"Ow!" Machiavelli cried. "What the fuck, man?"

Lord Byron glared at him, then turned and resumed the hike along the dark, uneven trail. Behind him, his crew muttered to one another. The words, "Screw him, let's go back," were half-heartedly uttered. Then, after a moment of indecision, they began to follow him once again, though cautiously now.

Lord Byron's face was carved into a malignant frown. He'd thought his first two stays at this shitty school were bad. But this was shaping up to be worse than either of them. He'd struck out twice with a poor white trash girl who should have been begging for his cock. Mr.

Partridge had mocked him with surprising acuity in math class. And his roommate had turned out to be the Korean kid whose dinner he stole when he arrived yesterday. The jerk had no sense of humor about it: he spent their first night together glaring at him balefully and growling in Korean. Standing in line for breakfast this morning, Lord Byron had been complaining to Jez that his roomie didn't speak a word of English, and the asshole smugly piped up, "I speak English. But not to you, motherfucker."

And now, he'd been kicked out of the dance.

He'd never been kicked out of a dance.

And by Mr. Lark, of all people. How fucking dare he.

He slashed his stick viciously, taking little satisfaction from its impact on the unseen brush. Up ahead, the undergrowth abruptly opened up, the path widened, and before him lay the lake, shining in the moonlight like an enormous coin. Saint Augustine, Machiavelli, and Hemlock whooped and shoved past him, galloping toward it.

"Let's make the skinny dipping!" Hemlock yelled, as Saint Augustine put Machiavelli in a headlock and tried to wrestle him down to the gritty mud at the water's edge.

They looked like cavorting imps in the silver-blue reflection of moonbeams off the still waters.

Stupid kids.

Lord Byron shook his head irritably and stepped into the shadow of a large tree to pee. Alone, the shouts of his friends reverberating off the water below and the rockface above, he reflected upon the favor that had brought him here once again. The gamble, as the headmistress called it. For the first time since he'd agreed to do it, he felt a twinge of doubt.

Had he made a huge mistake?

He'd figured he would breeze back to school, flash a few smiles, and dominate the situation effortlessly. He was a grown man now, after all. Instead, it was just like it was when he was fourteen. And sixteen. Frustrating, demeaning, and soul-crushingly boring.

A crackle of branches from behind him jerked him out of his reverie. Still peeing, he perked up and listened.

Twigs snapped rhythmically.

His pals were at the water's edge, goofing around and splashing each other. They were nowhere near the brush.

Someone was coming.

Before Lord Byron could utter a warning, his friends heard the dangerous sound, too. Their heads went up like prey animals. Another crunch of brush and they fled, abandoning him.

Goddamn it! It was New York all over again. Ditched dick out, in mid-piss, by his asshole friends. Assholes who wouldn't lift a finger to get him out of trouble, just like these particular assholes. Except this time, he wasn't high as balls on coke.

Alarmed, all he could do was duck behind the tree and crouch low, praying the shadows would conceal him.

If you were caught outside the school after curfew...

He watched, frozen with terror, as two figures emerged from the path. He sucked in his breath, afraid to so much as blink.

The two walked slowly to the water's edge. Saint Augustine, Machiavelli, and Hemlock were long gone, but it didn't appear as if the newcomers were searching for them. They continued walking, heading for the dock that stretched invitingly over the luminous water. They stepped onto it, paced the old wooden planks to the midpoint, and turned to face each other.

Lord Byron's mouth fell open.

It was Mr. Lark and Beryl.

He let go of his dick and stood in shock, unable to stop himself.

What the hell were they doing here?

He could see their mouths moving rapidly, silhouetted like shadow puppets against the shimmery blue of the lake and the glittery black of the night sky. He stuffed himself into his pants, crept around the tree, and strained to listen.

He couldn't hear a word they were saying.

Then, to his astonishment, they kissed.

"Ben—" she began.

"I've never stopped loving you," he said, stroking her hair. "Even after seven years."

Their lips met. It was just like he remembered. Just like the first time when they were seventeen.

English class. Junior year. The late afternoon sun leaked through the dusty windowpanes like molten copper, transforming the soft strands of her hair into red and gold flames.

The bell rang, the students rushed out, the teacher soon followed.

She remained behind, scribbling away in a notebook at her desk. He remained behind, too, because she was there. He'd been trying to think of some way to strike up a conversation with her—hell, to just say hi, even—ever since his first day of school more than a week ago.

She was the most beautiful girl he'd ever seen.

Then, he thought of something.

"By the way," he said, packing up his books and papers, preparing to leave. "Happy birthday."

She smiled at him in surprise.

"How did you know it's my birthday?"

"I have my ways," he replied, smiling back at her.

The classroom was deserted. They were all alone.

They lingered for a quarter of an hour: he complimenting her report on Samuel Taylor Coleridge, she expertly steering the conversation back to him again and again and again.

Where did he live? What did he like to do for fun? Did he love writing as much as she did?

And he told her. He wasn't supposed to tell anyone, but he did.

He lived in the imposing mansion outside of town. He liked to read for fun. He loved writing, though maybe not as much as she did.

His name was Benjamin Wallace Newland. Yes, of *that* Newland family. His was just a minor branch: his father was a cousin of *those* Newlands, who were governors and White House cabinet members and billionaire business magnates. But yes, his family was…comfortable.

"Bullshit. You're loaded," she giggled. "I've seen the car that brings you to school. Long black car *and* a driver. Is it a limo, or something?"

It was a Rolls-Royce, but he just grinned weakly and shrugged.

This was dangerous territory and he knew it. But he didn't put a stop to it until she leaned closer to him, placed her hand on his, and asked, "Do you have a girlfriend?"

He abruptly hoisted his bag, gave her an awkward wave, and said, "See you tomorrow. Hope you get lots of presents."

It was dangerous because he wanted to kiss her.

He desperately wanted to kiss her.

But he couldn't. He wasn't supposed to socialize with anyone at this school. This plebeian public school, to which he'd been sent as a last resort.

She followed him out of the school, past the deserted football field, and through the nearly empty faculty parking lot. His father's car and driver were parked there, waiting for him.

"Hey," she called out.

He should have kept walking. But he didn't. He stopped and turned around.

"I know about you," she said.

His heart stopped.

"What do you know?" he said, his voice unsteady.

"I know it's not your fault," she said.

What she knew was that he'd been kicked out of eleven private academies and prep schools, five in the last year alone.

This place was the final stop before tutors and a disgraceful GED.

He was a bad kid.

That's what everyone said. And he believed it.

But she said it wasn't his fault.

He'd arrived at his local high school, legally obliged to accept everyone including bad kids, with a reputation and a nickname: School Shooter. He'd never so much as touched a gun in his life. It was his appearance. Long hair, black clothes, trench coat. Frequent bruises. Frequent black eyes. And his demeanor. He slouched at his desk at the very back of the classroom. He ate lunch alone. He never spoke. He avoided eye contact.

All the kids steered clear of him.

And he steered clear of them.

But she wasn't going to. That's what she told him that day.

"I think you're interesting," she said. "Want to do something on Saturday?"

He should have turned and walked away from her.

He should have turned and run away from her.

Instead, he took a step toward her.

Then another.

Then, they kissed.

That was the first time. There were many more times after that.

They snuck around. Actually, he snuck around and made her sneak with him. No one could know about them.

She was so different from anyone he had ever known. She was poor. Not poor like the scholarship kids at the private schools he'd attended, with their second-hand designer clothes, ski trips to Aspen instead of St. Moritz, and mid-tier Ivy League aspirations. She was poor like the employees of his father's mining company.

She drove her dad's truck to school, a rattling rig mounted with deer lights, permanent mud spatters, and a gun rack with a loaded hunting rifle. When he asked her about the rifle—was it for competitive skeet shooting?—she informed him that her dad got it in trade from a friend of a friend who got it from a guy who bought it at a pawn shop. It was one of many her dad owned for hunting.

For fun? He asked.

For meat, she replied. Without it, they would be hungry come winter.

She drove them, in her dad's truck with her dad's meat-hunting gun, to all their dates. He didn't have a car of his own, didn't even know how to drive. And there was no way he could use his father's town car.

Someone would find out about them if he did.

He was obsessive about secrecy. They couldn't talk to each other at school. No texting, no phone calls, no social media, no email. They didn't hang out with her friends. He never brought her to his house, never introduced her to his family.

She went along with this grudgingly, at first.

"I don't care who knows," she told him so many times. So many times when they were wrapped in each other's arms. So many times when their naked bodies were pressed close in the velvet darkness. So many times when he told her he loved her but they had to keep this thing of theirs a secret.

"I don't care who knows…"

Then she lost patience.

"You're ashamed of me," she accused one terrible rainy night when her frustration reached a boiling point. "Let's just break up and you can find a rich girl you don't have to hide."

He couldn't bear to lose her. Out of panic, he confessed the truth.

It wasn't because he was ashamed of her.

It was because of Patrick.

He'd told people about Patrick many times. Every few years, a concerned teacher or physician or social worker would pull him aside, sit him down, and ask him where he got the bruises. Who had given him the black eyes? Who had broken his nose, who had choked him so hard it left fingerprints that lasted for days? Was someone at home hurting him?

He always answered honestly.

Patrick had hit him. Patrick had pushed him down the stairs. Patrick had held him under the water of their pool until he lost consciousness. Patrick had chased him with a baseball bat, screaming that he would kill him. Patrick had broken his rib and his collarbone and given him a concussion.

Patrick was his older brother.

When the teacher or physician or social worker heard that his abuser was a child, just like him, they always reacted the same way. There was a pause as they absorbed this information. Then their eyes went soft with relief. The corners of their mouths twitched in gentle amusement. Boys and their roughhousing. Growing boys never knew their own strength. Boys will be boys. Then the previously grave cadence of their voices was replaced by a lilting lightness, and they told him that he and his brother should learn to resolve their conflicts by using their words. Sometimes they handed him a pamphlet on how to do that.

His parents were no different. They hand-waved it away. Patrick had a temper. But he was such a good boy. Ben had always been histrionic. Ben was a crybaby. Even when his brother knocked out his front tooth. Even when he broke his wrist. Even when they caught him holding a knife to his throat.

Nobody cared until he turned fifteen and began getting in fights at school. When a boy reminded him of Patrick—the cocky smirk, the complete disregard for others, the casual cruelty—instinctively he sought to protect himself. And another fancy private school would kick him out for fighting. Now, at age seventeen, nobody asked him if anyone was hurting him at home. His bruises and black eyes surely came from fights. He was a bad kid, after all.

If his brother found out he had a girlfriend, he'd do something terrible to her, just to hurt him. He'd done it before. He'd smashed his beloved toys. He'd torn up his favorite books. He'd killed his puppy.

He hated his older brother more than anyone in the world.

He told her all this. And she believed him.

She was the first person who believed him.

But it made everything a thousand times worse.

They didn't break up. Instead, she now seemed to be on a mission to help him stop the abuse. When he told her he loved her, she responded, "I'd rather you love yourself, Ben."

"I don't know how you put up with it," she would say.

"I would never let someone do that to me."

"If anyone hurt me like that, I'd kill him."

Kill him.

Kill him.

Kill him.

If he didn't do something, she wouldn't respect him. He was sure of that. She would break up with him if he didn't man up and…

Kill him.

He would do anything for her.

Anything.

Then, one night, it happened.

For months, he'd been staying late at school, sneaking around on the weekends, coming home in the wee hours. For months, his brother demanded to know what he was up to. One evening, Ben was sitting in the rusty bed of her dad's pickup truck, waiting for her to come out of the school's newspaper office where she was working late. He remembered gazing up at a sky choked with clouds. There was not a star to be seen. That was all he remembered to this day. Except for a series of still images, snippets of sound, appalling sensations.

His brother's bright yellow Maserati rolling up. The mocking laugh. Patrick's fist striking his face. Her horrified cry. His brother grabbing her arm and twisting it, her phone falling to the pavement.

He shouting, "Leave her alone!"

His brother sneering, "Make me."

Hot, implacable anger kindling within him.

The rifle in the rack. Then in his hands. Then pointed at Patrick's face.

"Do it."

He heard her say, "Do it."

He remembered she said, "Do it…"

Didn't she?

Seven years later, here they were again. But this time, the sky was clear and filled with stars. The moon was shining down on them. And his brother was long dead.

He'd been certain he would never see her again.

"What happened to you?" she asked, as their lips parted. "You just disappeared."

"It was a scandal," he said, holding her in his arms as tight as Lord Byron had on the dance floor. "I was sent to Scandal School."

He'd protected her. After he stopped shaking, after his vision cleared, he told her to get in her dad's truck and drive away. As fast as she could. Go someplace with a lot of people who knew her, establish an alibi. Leave the gun.

She resisted, then complied.

"We don't know each other," he said.

It was the last thing he ever said to her.

When the police arrived, he told them he got the rifle from a friend of a friend who got it from a guy who bought it at a pawn shop. He had been alone when he shot his brother.

The scandal was huge. Two brothers: one shot the other for no discernible reason at school.

At school…a school shooter with one victim—his brother!

A tale as old as time. Cain and Abel. But with an irresistible twist: they were scions of the illustrious Newland family. Governor

Newland could not be reached for comment…not yet, at least. Paparazzi were camped out at the governor's mansion, awaiting a statement.

Nobody connected him with her, thanks to the secrecy he'd insisted upon. He was recalled by teachers and fellow students as a loner. She kept quiet, like he told her to. Her friends and family knew nothing about him. His father called upon all the Newland clan's power and influence to get him charged not with murder but with involuntary manslaughter. The story they fed the press was that young Ben, a troubled boy, had gone to the school to kill himself. His beloved big brother got wind of it and tried to stop him. The gun went off accidentally. It was a genuine tragedy.

But it was still manslaughter, and there was still a criminal charge and a plea bargain. And the scandal simply wouldn't die. The press—especially *Scandalicious News*, a fledgling gossip blog at the time—kept digging and digging and digging.

The story seemed fake.

There had to be more to it.

Maybe drugs were involved.

It was probably a fight over a girl.

Clearly his powerful family was protecting him in order to hide a dark secret. Probably financial malfeasance. Or something political. Maybe a scandal involving the White House!

Then one morning, an hour before dawn, a black van pulled up outside his house. He was blindfolded and loaded into it. Countless hours later, he arrived in the valley.

"Why are you still here?" she asked, running her fingers down his face, fingering the beard he grew when he started teaching full-time in hopes it would make him look like an authority figure.

"I don't know," he replied. "When I turned eighteen, the headmistress called me into her office and told me I couldn't leave. She gave me two options: go work on one of the farms, or become a teacher. I always hated manual labor."

He loosened the confining clasp of his arms so he could gaze down at her.

"But what are *you* doing here?" he asked. "What the hell are you doing here?"

She lowered her eyes.

"I volunteered," she said. "There's a boy. His name is Logan Asher Wyatt. He's the subject of a scandal—something involving the FBI. Logan told an anonymous source at *Scandalicious News* about a school that the elite send their kids to when they want to hide them from the press. I was sent here to find out if the school really exists. My cover story is that I'm a seventeen-year-old girl who's hiding out until my own scandal dies down."

"But you're not seventeen," he said. "You're twenty-four."

"I'm short. I've got a baby face. I get carded every time I buy liquor. I can pass for a teenager," she replied.

"But," he insisted. "Why you? Do you work for the FBI?"

"No," she said.

"Then why? Tell me the truth."

In his arms, she stiffened. She looked away from him: at the sky, at the lake, at the wooden planks of the dock. Anywhere but his face.

"I'm a reporter," she admitted. "I work for...um..."

"For who?" he demanded.

"Scandalicious News."

His body went numb. His arms fell to his sides, releasing her from their embrace. He took a step away from her.

"I'm going to be a famous writer one day," she always used to say. "Pulitzer Prize winning journalist Margot York."

"How..." he choked, his throat constricting as if hands were clenched around it. "How could you work for a filthy gossip site like that?"

"I—"

"They're the reason I got sent here, Margot!" he shouted.

"I didn't want to!" she cried. "I wanted to be a real journalist. It was the only place that would give me an internship in college, the only place that would hire me after I graduated."

"Pulitzer Prize winning journalist Margot York," he said mockingly.

"It's only temporary," she insisted, reaching out to touch his arm. "I just need to break a big story—a real story, like this—and I'll be able to get a job as a real journalist. This school...it's not just tabloid gossip. It's a huge international…"

"Scandal?" he said bitterly

"Scandal. Yes," she replied.

He folded his arms over his chest.

"How did you do it?" he demanded. "How did you get in?"

"There have been rumors about this place for years. A certain senator's name came up when I was working on a story about another kid who disappeared right at the height of their scandal. The publisher of *Scandalicious News,* he…persuaded the senator that if he didn't get me in here, a story about a sex tape starring the two of us would be front page news. The senator arranged everything. I have no idea how he did it. I just was told to be ready to get kidnapped and brought to the school. And that's exactly what happened."

"Is there really a sex tape?" he demanded.

"What?" she said.

"Did you really have sex with the senator, or did you just threaten to publish a false story saying you did?"

He could hear the jealousy in his voice. It was absurd. Of all the things to be upset about at a time like this…

"*Scandalicious News* has worse dirt on him than sex with a seventeen-year-old," she said. "Believe me. I'm sure the sex tape was just the thin end of the wedge."

He grabbed her by the shoulders and thrust his face within an inch of hers.

"Did you have sex with him?" he shouted.

"What the hell is wrong with you?" she shouted back.

She pried his hands off her shoulders and glared up at him.

"You haven't changed at all, have you? Jesus Christ, Ben! You're a grown man—"

"And you're a grown woman pretending to be a teenager!"

"Yeah, *pretending*! You're not pretending at all. It's like you're still seventeen! Didn't you grow up at all in the past seven years?"

He opened his mouth to retort, but no sound came out.

His feelings were all mixed up. Longing, resentment, anger, love. Just like when he was seventeen.

Maybe Margot was right. Maybe he never grew up.

And maybe he never could.

He'd been stuck in this valley, this unnatural simulacrum of real life, for seven years. Wasn't it possible he was also trapped by the erratic emotions and dubious instincts of a teenager?

He thought she hadn't changed since he last saw her.

He was wrong.

He was the one who hadn't changed.

A rustling sound in the bushes near the trailhead stopped him dead.

"We have to go," he said, grabbing her arm.

She threw off his hand, her eyes flashing with rage.

"Don't touch—"

"I'm serious, someone's coming!" he whispered.

She let him take her arm then, and together the two of them darted down the dock toward the path leading to the school. He glanced behind him, then they plunged into the brush.

Lord Byron emerged from behind the tree. He stared at the shadowy entrance to the secret trail, then at the deserted dock. Slowly, he picked his way out of the underbrush and shook his head in amazement.

Try as he might, he hadn't been able to catch a word of their conversation, but it looked intense.

Actually...he'd heard one thing quite clearly:

Mr. Lark shouting, "Did you have sex with him?"

And her angry reply, "What the hell is wrong with you?"

He let out a chuckle of wonder. The girl really did like older men. And she got around. Fast.

He almost admired her. And he forgave Mr. Lark for his dickish treatment of him tonight.

Did you have sex with him? Clearly, "him" meant "Lord Byron."

The man was dying of jealousy.

He brushed twigs and dry leaves off his trousers, gave the lake a final glance, and started up the path toward the school.

He would have Beryl. That was a certainty now.

78

He had all the leverage he needed to make her be with him. It was going to be fun watching her squirm.

Chapter 7

It was Saturday. Margot—who was already responding automatically to her new name, Beryl—spent the morning in the school library trying to brush up on nearly forgotten facts she'd learned in high school seven years ago.

The place was an antiquarian's dream. Two stories of heirloom-quality tomes that would fetch a hefty fee on the auction block at Christie's. Atlases from the colonial era when Ethiopia was called Abyssinia, Namibia was called Damaraland, and Liberia was called Liberia, much to her surprise. Math textbooks with story problems about horse-drawn carriages and steamboats. Physics books that proposed the potential for a journey to the moon sometime in the next hundred years.

Margot—no, Beryl now—was a creature of the internet. Now, shelves upon shelves of encyclopedias were her Wikipedia. A dusty card catalog was her search engine. And her newsfeed was a century out of date.

At noon, she gave up. She had a bachelor's degree from a decent state college. She shouldn't be stymied by basic high school curricula. It was (privately, thank God) humiliating.

The scent of freshly baked bread and savory meat drifted out of the open doors of the dining hall next to the library, calling to her. She couldn't get over how good the food was here. The dining hall was nothing like the cafeterias she'd endured as a teenager. Or a college student. Or even an employee of America's most reputable (ha) gossip publication. She hadn't been able to afford an Ivy League education, but the high ceilings, the soaring windows, the polished floors and elegant oil paintings and unblemished wooden tables fit every fantasy she'd ever had of what such an experience would have been like, aesthetically speaking.

She grabbed a tray (even the trays were chic, with a muted mid-century color scheme) and got in line. In front of her stood Poe, their spine rigid. Beryl opened her mouth to greet her roommate, but before she could, a familiar face interposed itself between hers and the back of Poe's head.

"Hey there," Lord Byron said, flashing her the self-satisfied smile that the photogs of *Scandalicious News* had perfectly captured during his first trial. "Eat fast. After lunch, I'm taking you to the movies in town."

Beryl blinked at him in surprise.

"Well, color me astonished," she said.

His smile slipped just a fraction.

"What do you mean?" he said.

"I'm shocked there's a movie theater in town. And that we're allowed to go to town," she said.

Poe turned in line and peered around Lord Byron's broad shoulder.

"We can leave the school grounds on Saturdays and Sundays. But only if we behave," they added, casting a withering glance at the young man.

"*The Lost Boys* is playing," Lord Byron continued, as if Poe hadn't spoken. He reached out a finger and touched the half-hickey he'd managed to suck into Beryl's neck last night. "Love bites. Your favorite."

"Aw, too bad, Lord Byron," a voice declared. "Beryl already agreed to spend the day with us."

Shōnagon, flanked by two girls and a boy, strode up to the food service line. She and the three kids held fully loaded trays and wore contentious frowns.

"With the newspaper nerds? You can't be serious," Lord Byron said.

"Come on, Beryl. We're doing family-style lunch today," Shōnagon informed Lord Byron rather than Beryl. She grabbed her arm and tugged her out of the line.

Lord Byron shook his head, his full lips curling up in a sardonic grin that did little to hide the irritation that flashed in his eyes.

"Last chance," he called out as Beryl was hustled away by the members of the newspaper club.

"Go to the back of the line. No cuts," Poe ordered.

The tip of Lord Byron's tongue made a slow circle against the inside of his cheek as he glared down at Poe.

"Catch you later," he growled at the headmistress's personal tattletale, then sauntered away.

"You're welcome," Shōnagon said, guiding Beryl to a large, round table beside one of the windows.

"You didn't have to," Beryl said as the kids set down their trays and began arranging the food into a Thanksgiving-style spread at the center of the table.

"He's such an asshole," exclaimed one of the girls, who looked to be no more than fourteen, as she doled out empty plates.

"He is pig," the other girl replied. She had a Slavic accent. Maybe Russian. Beryl couldn't tell.

"At least you can avoid him," Charlemagne said. "I have to live with the motherfucker. I hate him!"

"I hate him more," the Slavic girl retorted.

"I don't even know him, and I already hate him," the fourteen-year-old girl said.

"You guys are the newspaper club?" Beryl interjected.

"Yes, we are!" Shōnagon beamed.

As one, they all sat and began passing around plates heaped with food.

"Charlemagne is our typesetter and printer," Shōnagon said, pointing at the boy. "Electra is our proofreader."

The Slavic girl gave Beryl a nod.

"And Thoreau is our editor-in-chief," she concluded, indicating the youngest girl. "I'm the columnist, like I told you the other night, but we all write articles. Mr. Lark is our publisher."

Mr. Lark.

Ben.

Beryl could feel her face turning red. She accepted a bowl of edamame and concentrated very hard on spooning the emerald-green pods onto her plate.

"He's really nice," Charlemagne said.

"Yes, that's what Shōnagon told me," Beryl murmured.

"He is really handsome," Electra said.

"Really, *really* handsome," Thoreau giggled. "But he should get rid of the beard. It makes him look old."

"I have no opinion," Charlemagne countered, waggling his eyebrows. "I prefer the ladies."

The girls giggled. Beryl shoveled pan-seared scallops onto her plate and prayed they would change the subject.

If anything was going to give away her secret, it was her feelings about Mr. Lark.

"This is the only road to town?" Beryl asked as she, Shōnagon, Electra, Thoreau, and Charlemagne set out half an hour later.

"Yep," said Shōnagon. "I wish there were cars here. I hate walking in these shoes. I always get blisters on my big toes."

It was an idyllic country road, unpaved but smooth, its surface well-trodden. On both sides, tall grass and bright wildflowers with tattered petals waved in the wind. To the south, she could see farmland: wide open fields of green herbage, rustic red barns, and tiny quadrupedal dots that might have been cows or horses. To the north was the lake, where she and Ben had talked last night.

Talked and kissed.

Straight ahead to the east lay their destination: the town.

"How far is it?" she asked.

"Like, a mile, I think?" said Shōnagon.

"One and a half miles," Electra corrected. "Maybe a bit less."

The valley was deep: a U-shaped cleft between the rugged mountains that surrounded it on all sides. It was shaped like an almond or an eye: extremely narrow at the northern and southern ends, wide in the middle. She guessed it stretched eight miles from tip to tip, its width possibly three miles. The place was lush with plant life, but the trees were stunted and clustered primarily at the base of the rockface. They were all, she noted, evergreen. Not deciduous. Deciduous trees might have helped her figure out what season it was here and, in turn, which hemisphere the valley occupied.

Beryl wished she had a notebook to record these details. She usually took notes using an app on her phone. But she had access to neither phones nor apps here. How the hell did reporters do it back in the days before the internet? Did they all have phenomenal memories?

Suddenly, Shōnagon's previous comment—"I wish there were cars here"—struck Beryl.

"Don't the teachers have cars?" she asked.

"No. Nobody has a car," said Shōnagon.

"There's no cars or buses or anything," said Thoreau.

"Just our natural hooves," Charlemagne quipped, lifting his feet high to prance in a cartoonish trot.

As it turned out, motorized vehicles weren't the only thing the valley lacked. As they approached the town, Beryl tipped her head back to look at the sky, which was clear and blue…and unobstructed by power lines.

She contemplated the coterie of identical one-story cottages that stood at the terminus of the road. They lay in perfectly straight rows bisected by wide sidewalks, their tidy lawns surrounded by actual white picket fences, a picture book Levittown. There was not a utility pole in sight.

"Where are the telephone poles?" she asked.

"There's no phones," said Charlemagne.

"No electricity, either?" Beryl asked.

"Of course there's electricity," Shōnagon laughed. "How do you think the movie theater shows movies?"

"But—" Beryl began.

"The electrical cables are buried underground. That's what Ms. Starling told us in science," said Thoreau. "There's a small power plant out past the farms, by the air strip."

"Wow," Beryl said. "Can we go see it?"

The kids stared at her.

"No," Shōnagon scoffed. "It's just a boring concrete building."

"We're not allowed anywhere except school and town," said Electra.

"Why the hell would you want to see the power plant?"

Charlemagne demanded.

"I don't know…never mind," Beryl muttered.

She decided the best thing to do was keep her eyes open and her mouth shut. At least for the time being.

The cottages gave way to a wide, generous street with shops on both sides. The street was paved with cobblestones. Beryl shook her head in wonder. Why not? There were no cars whose shocks and struts could be damaged. And the effect was quaint as hell.

"That's the grocery, that's the tailor. We're not allowed in those," Thoreau said, pointing out two buildings on the western side of the street.

The group crossed to the eastern side. The sidewalk was as smooth as marble and immaculately clean. They passed a fancy restaurant with a sign that read "La Cage Dorée," a bookstore called Vogelhaus Books, and a coffee shop that looked incredibly inviting to caffeine-starved Beryl that bore the name Caffè Nido. Next to the coffee shop stood a small movie theater: The Columbarium, according to the marquee out front, which promised a double feature of *Pretty in Pink* and *The Lost Boys*.

"Let's pick our seats before all the good ones get taken, then we'll get popcorn," said Charlemagne, charging toward the double doors situated opposite an old-fashioned ticket window. "No, popcorn first," Electra and Thoreau chorused, hot on his heels.

"Wait," Beryl said, grabbing the sleeve of Shōnagon's blazer.

"What's wrong?" Shōnagon asked.

"Um. I don't have any money," Beryl confessed.

"Why would you need money?" Shōnagon said. "It's free."

"Really?"

"Everything's free in town."

"Everything?" Beryl repeated. "Not literally everything?"

Shōnagon just laughed.

"You're so funny!" she said, tugging Beryl through the theater doors.

Inside, Beryl found two surprises. First, the single-screen movie house looked like a retro mall theater frozen in time, with gaudy twentieth-century movie posters, frenetic carpeting, and a glass-fronted concession stand. And second, Lord Byron was lounging by the popcorn machine, a sly smirk on his handsome face.

He said nothing, but his eyes devoured Beryl as she approached the concession stand and obtained a bag of popcorn from a deadpan employee. Shōnagon and Charlemagne got popcorn flavored with flakes of nori seaweed. Thoreau chose the garam masala version. Electra refused any flavors at all, including the classic butter and salt that Beryl had opted for.

"I only eat it naked," she said, sending Charlemagne into a fit of guffaws.

"Absolute last chance," Lord Byron murmured as Beryl trailed the newspaper club into the theater. It took all her willpower to keep her eyes pointed straight ahead and her face neutral.

"This is gonna be so fun!" Shōnagon enthused, bouncing on her seat after four attempts by the group to find the perfect spots in the center row. "I like the girl that stars in this."

"You mean Molly Ringwald?"

"Yeah, her. They showed *Sixteen Candles* two weeks ago, and *The Breakfast Club* a week before that. She's really funny. Like you."

Beryl had never considered Molly Ringwald to be a comedic genius. But then again, Shōnagon seemed to have a weird sense of humor. Perhaps she should be flattered?

Gradually the theater filled with kids, as well as a few adults who sat in the back. Beryl craned her neck, trying to figure out who they were. They weren't teachers from the school, nor did she recognize them from the dining hall staff. She scrutinized their clothing for clues, then her gaze landed on Lord Byron. He sat surrounded by a gang of kids: the boys he'd stormed out of the dance with, and the girls she had seen him flirting with the night she arrived at the school. His eyes immediately locked on hers and a grin blossomed like a poisonous flower on his lips.

Quickly she turned away to face the screen. Still, she could feel his eyes on her. It made the hairs on the back of her neck stand up.

Mercifully, the lights dimmed and the movie began. Beryl had never seen *Pretty in Pink* before. It was way, way before her time. Her mother adored it, though, and had often tried to coax her into watching. It was even duller than she'd imagined. Shōnagon and the rest of the kids in the theater seemed entranced by it, however.

No internet, no TV, no cars, and nowhere to go besides a curious little town…they must be starved for entertainment. She wondered how long it would take for her to be similarly thrilled by slight joys. Luckily, she wouldn't be here long enough to find out.

During the intermission between films, Shōnagon leaned over and whispered to Beryl, "Are you poor like her?"

"Like who?"

"Molly Ringwald."

Beryl, nonplussed, whispered back, "I guess so."

Shōnagon seemed pleased by this. She patted Beryl's hand sympathetically.

"I would've bought you a nice prom dress," she said. "Couture. Not a crappy used rag like her friend gave her."

"Thanks?" Beryl said. "That's very…generous of you."

This seemed to please Shōnagon even more. Then the lights dimmed once again and *The Lost Boys* began.

Underage vampires, a strange song about incest, Kiefer Sutherland's attempt as an adult to portray a teen (that hit a little too close to home for her taste). It was the kind of thing she and Ben would have enjoyed ironically when they were kids. She could picture it: sitting in the back row, whispering mocking comments, gradually abandoning the narrative to make out with ever-increasing passion.

She must not think about Ben. Ben was gone. In his place was Mr. Lark, a man she didn't know. Nor did he know her. They were strangers to each other.

Weren't they?

When the credits rolled and the lights came up, the theater erupted in applause.

"That was so, so good!" Shōnagon squealed. "Wasn't that good?"

Electra, Thoreau, and Charlemagne replied in the affirmative. Beryl merely smiled.

"Let's go get a drink!" Shōnagon suggested.

A drink was the one thing Beryl had been dying for ever since she arrived in this peculiar valley. However, she was pretty sure liquor wasn't what Shōnagon had in mind.

She trailed the newspaper club and the rest of the movie-goers out of the theater. As she passed Lord Byron's row, she felt fingers pluck at her wool skirt.

"Sparkly vampires," he murmured suggestively, licking his upper lip.

She yanked the fabric out of his grasp and hurried up the aisle.

God, he unnerved her.

She needed to find a way to deal with him. The story was the school: that's how she planned to write it. But he was the framing device. A recap of the Notorious L.A.W.'s past scandals and mysterious vanishing acts, culminating in his third scandal and disappearance. Her intrepid quest to discover where he'd gone. Then a meaty two-thousand-word piece about the school: its purpose, its student body, and most important, its secret location.

The latter was proving unexpectedly difficult to ascertain. She still hadn't the foggiest clue where she was. A remote mountain range in China? The Andes, somewhere between Argentina and Chile? The Rocky Mountains just outside Denver, Colorado?

In any event, Lord Byron had turned out to be an unexpected obstacle to journalistic success. She was rarely intimidated—she could jostle paparazzi and tabloid reporters out of the way for a story, ambush unsuspecting private citizens, and absorb vituperative insults with the best of them. But Lord Byron was throwing her for a loop.

It was because he was a kid. He may have just turned eighteen, but he was definitely still a boy. A boy who was appallingly horny for her. Had he been an adult, she would have used that to her advantage. Let him grope her breasts, maybe fondle him a little. But she couldn't possibly do that. Just thinking about it made her feel like a pedophile.

Outside, the sun was sinking behind the rock wall on the other side of the valley, illuminating the school with fiery tongues of red and yellow. The students spilled out onto the sidewalk, laughing and talking. Around them, the town seemed unnaturally quiet. It wasn't just the absence of truck motors and car engines. As she and her new friends strolled the main drag, she realized why. Not a single dog was barking. Nobody was out walking their dogs, either. She wondered if pets were yet another thing that was forbidden in the valley.

"Let's go to the park," said Charlemagne.

"No, Caffè Nido," said Electra.

"I vote Caffè Nido," said Shōnagon.

"What's Coffee Needle?" Beryl inquired.

Shōnagon burst out laughing.

"You are *so* funny!" she cried, threading her arm through Beryl's and leading her down the sidewalk. They didn't go far. Right next door to the movie theater was the coffee shop, Caffè Nido.

The decor was deliciously cozy. Velvet-upholstered couches and intimate cafe tables were scattered throughout the warm, just-dim-enough space, which was lit by antique wall sconces that looked like real candles. The walls were exposed brick interspersed with built-in shelves loaded with books and board games. The counter was a tasteful riot of top-of-the-line espresso machines, dainty pastries under glass domes, and enormous burlap bags of coffee beans stamped with the words "Brazil," "Hawaii," and "Indonesia."

The place was doing brisk business, but the line moved quickly.

"Is everything free here, too?" Beryl joked as Shōnagon stepped up to the counter and considered the baked goods.

"Of course," she replied. "I told you, everything's free."

Shōnagon ordered a red bean daifuku and a beignet, along with a cup of hot chocolate. Charlemagne asked for a balushahi and a berliner. Electra ordered an espresso. Thoreau opted for two tartelettes au citron.

Each of them received what they requested. None of them were charged.

"Wow," Beryl murmured under her breath. Then, aloud, she ventured, "Can I have black coffee? The biggest you've got?"

After a moment, the barista handed her an enormous mug brimming with hot, obsidian liquid. It smelled heavenly. She, too, was not charged.

A girl could get used to a place like this, she thought.

"You know what?" Shōnagon said, biting into her beignet after they'd crammed themselves around the only free table in the coffee shop. "I kind of wanna do a column about today."

"Like what?" said Electra, sipping primly at her tiny cup.

"Like, about the movie. Not the vampire one. The one with Molly Ringwald. Or maybe about all her movies."

"How many words do you think you can write about that?"

inquired Thoreau, her editor-in-chief.

"Lots. Maybe three hundred."

"Just don't give it to me so late this time," Charlemagne said. "I had to stay up after midnight setting the type for your last column."

Beryl felt a swell of amusement listening to the newspaper club discuss their upcoming edition. They sounded just like her coworkers sitting around the bar after work. Minus a quiverful of stinging personal insults and some truly grotesque profanity, of course.

The last time she'd spent an evening talking shop like this, she'd been the subject of all conversation and the guest of honor. The day before she was kidnapped, the *Scandalicious News* reporting team took her out for a final fete. Gracing them with his presence was founder and publisher Baz Bennigan: red-faced, rotund, and resolutely Australian.

"Here's to Margot," he boomed, raising his half-drunk beer (he was, himself, half-drunk as well). "Heading off to perilous parts unknown in the tradition of stunt journalist Nellie Bly. I salute you: a ripper scandalmonger with the most incredible breasts—"

"That you've never seen!" Margot interjected, laughing.

"And never will!" the political news reporter added.

"To Margot! No..." Baz amended. "To Nellie Bly. That's your code name. Secret missions require code names. To Nellie!"

Her colleagues raised their glasses and chorused, "To Nellie!"

At the time, she'd been flattered by the comparison. But now, it was beginning to make her anxious.

Nellie Bly made a name for herself by posing as a mentally ill woman and getting herself committed to an insane asylum for ten days, with a promise from her publisher that he would get her back out once her investigation was done.

Margot had agreed to a similar scheme without any reservations. But now that she was here, going by the name Beryl and trapped in a mysterious valley, she was starting to have doubts. Baz was no golden-age-of-journalism newspaperman. He was a glorified blogger, social media butterfly, and gossip whore with an inordinate appetite for alcohol and a natural capriciousness that bordered on utter irresponsibility.

What if her publisher couldn't get her out?

At that moment, another publisher—the school newspaper's publisher—interrupted her disquieting reverie. A bell jingled, the door swung open, and Mr. Lark entered the coffee shop. He strode to the counter, handed the barista a stainless steel travel mug, and said, "The usual, please."

He leaned against the counter and idly surveyed the crowd, perhaps searching for a place to sit. He looked tired. And troubled.

Deeply troubled.

They hadn't seen each other since parting ways in the dim hall outside Beryl's dorm room last night. He'd touched her bare shoulder, his fingers brushing the goosebumps that the cold night air had raised, then he turned away and vanished into the darkness.

His eyes came to rest on Beryl's. She tried to pull her gaze away from his, but she couldn't. She could feel the touch of his fingers on her skin…could feel his lips—

"Hey Mr. Lark!" Charlemagne called out, waving.

Mr. Lark's features instantly rearranged themselves into a benign, professorial smile. He accepted the full travel mug from the barista, then made his way to the table where his students sat.

"Well, how are my cub reporters?" he said.

"We went to the movies! It was so fun," said Shōnagon. "I think I might do a column on the films of Molly Ringwald. Like, an overview-thing."

"Interesting," he commented. "A career retrospective."

"I think she should do a food column instead," said Thoreau. "Maybe a review of last week's dinners. We could run it beside next week's menu. Almost like a food section. Get it?"

"I do," Mr. Lark said. "Another interesting idea."

As the kids chattered at him, Beryl caught his eye.

"Hazelnut latte, two-percent milk?" she inquired sotto voce.

He nodded.

"Nothing changes," she murmured.

His jaw tightened.

"Well," he said. "I don't want to interrupt your Saturday night. Have fun, people. And make sure you do your homework. You have a test on Monday, Thoreau. And you, Charlemagne—"

"I know, I know—it's done. I forgot to turn it in is all."

His newspaper staff called out farewells as he opened the door and gave them a parting wave. As he stepped out, another figure glided in behind him.

Electra and Thoreau let out groans. Charlemagne emitted a string of Korean words that had the unmistakable cadence of profanity.

"Why the hell won't he just give up?" Shōnagon muttered.

It was Lord Byron.

Again.

He marched up to the table, ignored everyone but Beryl, and announced, "I'm taking you to dinner. At the restaurant. Right now."

Beryl blinked in surprise.

He certainly was persistent.

She opened her mouth to say no, then hesitated.

Actually…she should accept. He couldn't grope her in a restaurant. They could talk privately, unimpeded by his boner. She could ask him why the FBI was after him. She could find out the truth about his scandal.

"You are not taking her anywhere," said Electra.

"Can't you see she's busy?" said Thoreau.

"Keojyeo!" rumbled Charlemagne.

"Beryl," Lord Byron said, holding out his hand and raising one eyebrow. "Let's go."

She considered his hand. She started to reach for it.

"Go away!" Shōnagon snapped.

She put her hand protectively on Beryl's and glared up at him.

Reluctantly, Beryl shook her head at Lord Byron.

"No, thank you," she replied. "I'm with my friends."

Lord Byron eyed her for a long moment. He knocked on the tabletop with the knuckle of his index finger, smirked, and sauntered away without another word. The little bell jingled as the door opened. Beryl braced herself for a slam, but it shut softly behind him.

Electra met Beryl's eyes. She let out a tense breath.

"He is pig," she said.

"I hate him. I hate him so much!" Charlemagne growled, then he began to mutter under his breath in Korean once again.

"You've gotta be careful, Beryl. If someone takes you to the restaurant, that means you're on a date," Shōnagon informed her.

"So, if I took the four of you to the restaurant right now, all of us would be on a date with each other?" Beryl inquired, grinning.

The kids glanced at each other, then burst out laughing.

"Yes!" Charlemagne crowed. "Orgy date! I've been wanting one forever—let's go, girls!"

She giggled along with Shōnagon, Electra, and Thoreau, then opened her mouth to crack another joke when suddenly, from somewhere outside in the darkness, a low note like a foghorn sounded. Instantly, the comfortable buzz of conversation in the coffee shop ceased. Cups clattered against saucers, silverware clanged to the floor, and each and every person abruptly sprang to their feet.

"What? What's happening?" Beryl asked, as Shōnagon, Charlemagne, Electra, and Thoreau abandoned their food and bolted for the door.

"Hurry!" Shōnagon cried, stretching out her arm and seizing Beryl by the hand. "We have to go!"

"Go where?" Beryl exclaimed as she was pulled through the door, the bodies of the other patrons heaving against hers.

Out on the sidewalk, students swarmed out of the restaurant and bookstore. Others came running from the park north of the movie theater. All of them were dashing toward the road that led back to the school. She caught sight of Lord Byron; even he was sprinting as if in fear of his life, the normally arrogant expression on his face replaced by one of anxiety.

"Shōnagon," Beryl wheezed as her friend dragged her along the dirt path (Mr. Cassowary was right—she had no stamina). "What's happening?"

"That was the curfew warning," she replied. "It blew earlier than usual. I don't know why."

"So?"

"So? So you don't want to be caught off school grounds after curfew!" Shōnagon exclaimed.

"Why? What'll happen?"

Shōnagon didn't reply. She just drove her feet harder and faster into the ground.

"Tell me," Beryl panted. "What happens if you break curfew?"

Shōnagon glanced over her shoulder at Beryl. Her face was painted with fear.

"You can end up in the aviary."

"What's the aviary?"

Shōnagon jerked Beryl's arm.

"Shut up, Beryl, and run!"

"So," said Poe, climbing into bed after Mr. Crane announced it was time for the students to retire for the night. "What did you do in town?"

Beryl sat on the edge of her mattress rubbing her feet, which were sore from the desperate dash up the dirt road. With a pang, she realized that Shōnagon had invited her in front of Poe, explicitly excluding them.

"Oh," she said, standing and reaching for her pajamas so she could avoid her roommate's eyes. "Nothing much. Went to the movies. Watched a couple '80s hits. Got some food afterward."

"Hm," Poe muttered. "Fun."

As Beryl pulled on her pajamas, she felt inexpressibly guilty. She'd forgotten how much being a teenager could suck. She should apologize.

No, it was too late for that.

She sighed and climbed into bed, pulling the covers up to her chin. She would simply do better next time.

But there wouldn't be a next time. Surely she would be back home before next Saturday.

"Poe?" she said. "Can I ask you something?"

Poe grunted noncommittally.

"What's the aviary?"

Poe was silent.

"It's where the bad kids live," they said at last.

"Bad kids?" Beryl grinned mirthlessly. "I thought we were the bad kids."

"All of us are here because we did something scandalous, like take drugs or send naked pictures of ourselves or get caught on camera saying racist stuff. Or we broke some kind of religious or cultural taboo. Non-violent scandals, understand?" Poe said. "The kids with violent scandals—the arsonists and rapists and murderers—they live in the aviary."

Beryl's blood ran cold and her stomach went sour.

"But what is it?"

"It's a secret wing of the school. None of us kids know where it is. Nobody's ever seen it. But there are rumors it's a dungeon. A real dungeon. And—" Poe snapped their mouth shut abruptly.

"What?" Beryl whispered.

"Some kids tried to find it once. A long time ago. They ran when they heard screams. Horrible screams. And there was one boy…" Poe's eyes slowly unfocused as they gazed at the far wall of the room. "One boy I knew, he got sent there. For breaking the rules."

"What happened to him?"

"I don't know," Poe said softly. "I never saw him again."

A light tap on the outside of the door made both of them jump.

"Lights out," Mr. Crane's voice called from the other side.

Poe reached for the bedside table. Their hand was shaking. They switched off the lamp. They didn't say good night.

Beryl lay on her back in the dark, staring at the unseen ceiling above.

It was horrifying.

Then she realized something.

The headmistress had been telling her the truth all along. There really were fifty-four students at the school.

The missing ten were locked away in a dungeon.

Beryl shivered and curled up on her side, wrapping her arms around her body as if to protect herself.

This school was more dangerous than she'd realized. She had to get the information she needed for her story and get the hell out.

Before it was too late.

Chapter 8

Sunlight was streaming through the bedroom window. Beryl had been awake for half an hour. Poe lay motionless, their face turned toward the wall.

"Hey Poe? You awake?" Beryl whispered from her bed.

Poe let out a groan.

"Whaddya want?"

"What are we supposed to do today?"

"Nothing. It's Sunday. We can sleep as late as we want," Poe mumbled irritably. "Which is what I plan to do."

And they pulled the covers over their head.

Beryl rolled out of bed and quietly donned her uniform. Besides the dress she'd worn to the dance and a gray sweatsuit she'd been given for gym class, the uniform was all the clothing she had: four skirts, four blouses, two blazers, and one tie. Apparently the headmistress didn't believe in lounge wear.

She crept out of the bedroom, shutting the door softly behind her. She walked down the hall, noting that nearly all of the other doors were closed as well.

After a desultory study session in the library, where she was the only soul hunched over a stack of outdated books, she rose, stretched, and wandered out to find something to eat.

Though it was nearly noon, only four students were in the dining hall, and they were all seated together at a table at the center of the room. The food service line was unstaffed and the kitchen was dark. In place of the usual trays of steaming food were wrapped bundles labeled "Sandwiches," "Salads," "Noodles/Rice," "Bento," and "Tiffin."

Beryl surreptitiously studied the quartet of girls as she selected a banh mi sandwich swaddled in brown paper. They were the same ones who had been seated with Lord Byron at the movies. They were stunningly pretty in a sorority-girls-without-makeup way. Only one of them was blonde, but they all exuded blonde energy.

Beryl started for a table across the room when the blonde beckoned to her.

"Sit with us," she said. She had a slight Southern accent.

As soon as Beryl heard her voice, she realized who she was. She was the girl at the dance who berated Poe about the punch. The one who helped Lord Byron get her on the dance floor so he could paw her.

"Um…" said Beryl.

The girl patted the empty seat next to her invitingly.

"All right," Beryl said uncertainly. "Thanks."

She approached, placed her sandwich on the table, and sat. The girls watched her intently. She cleared her throat, feeling distinctly uncomfortable.

"This is Medusa, Hecate, and Circe," the blonde girl said.

"Interesting names," Beryl replied.

"And I'm Jez," she said. She flashed Beryl the artful smile of a professional beauty contestant.

"These sandwiches any good?" Beryl asked, just for something to say, as she unwrapped her banh mi.

The four girls had thick books with black covers before them and no food.

Jez shook her head.

"The kitchen is closed on Sundays. We don't eat that stuff. We use this as our fasting day."

"To lose weight?" Beryl asked, taking a big bite.

"Do you think we need to lose weight?" the girl called Hecate inquired in a too-sweet voice.

Beryl shrugged. She wished she hadn't sat down with these girls. They were of a type. She'd done a story on their future selves a year ago: the Mormon Mommy Cam Girls. She'd received death threats for that one.

"Whatcha reading?" Beryl inquired, her mouth full.

"The Word," replied Medusa, folding her hands atop the cracked leather cover of her book.

That was when it dawned on her.

"You're the God Squad, right?" said Beryl.

The girls bristled visibly.

"That is an offensive term," Jez replied in a voice that was almost as tight as the hands that now clasped her Bible.

"I'm sorry," said Beryl. "I didn't realize."

Jez considered her for a long moment.

She unclasped her Bible. She reached out and grabbed Beryl's hand. She pressed it between both of hers and looked deep into her eyes.

"I forgive you," she said.

Beryl was too taken aback to speak.

Abruptly, Jez rose.

"All right!" she said. "Time to go."

"Where?" Beryl asked.

Jez gave her a cunning smile.

"Come and see," she replied.

Surely this was some scheme she and Lord Byron had cooked up. It was obvious. She'd been in cahoots with him before.

"Yeah…" Beryl said. "I think I'll pass."

"Aren't you even a little curious?" Jez said.

Beryl was indeed curious. More than a little curious. Extremely curious.

This girl had a strange charisma about her. She was…compelling. That was the word for it. Beryl had met few people who seemed so confident in their ability to *compel* you to obey. Jez was intriguing, to say the least.

"Okay," Beryl said, standing. "Lead the way."

She brought her sandwich along, nibbling at it as she and the God Squad hiked up the dirt road to town. She'd finished and was brushing the crumbs off her fingers when they reached the cottages.

The girls didn't say a word. They hadn't spoken from the moment they passed through the school's heavy iron gate. When Beryl tried to talk, she was fiercely shushed.

They wended their way through the miniature neighborhood and turned north onto the cobblestone-paved street. They strode up the main drag, past the coffee shop and movie theater. They walked through the small park with its graceful wrought iron benches and picturesque picnic tables. At the northern end of the park was a narrow trail leading into a grove of trees. An orchard. It was toward this that the God Squad bent their steps.

At the outer edge of the orchard, amid the heavily laden apple and pear trees, stood a simple, one-room interfaith chapel topped by a modest spire. Its roof was covered in wood shake and its clapboard siding was painted bone white. To Beryl's surprise, it was surrounded by a large crowd of kids and adults.

Some were leaning against the trees despite the fruit that hung, pendulous and sticky, from the low boughs. Others were clustered at the door in a loose queue. All of her junior-level classmates were there, along with the entire newspaper club and a number of students whom she'd only glimpsed in the dining hall and at the dance. Even Lord Byron was in attendance, lounging against the outside wall. He gave her a cocky grin when he spied her.

"Beryl!" Shōnagon exclaimed, jogging over. "I didn't see you at breakfast. I figured Poe trapped you with the big sleep. They get grumpy as hell if you wake them early on Sunday."

She threaded her arm through Beryl's and steered her toward a cluster of stumps out of earshot of Jez.

"How did the God Squad get their hands on you?" she asked. "You've got to stay away from them. They're ultra bitches. Ask Poe."

"Maybe they're just hungry," Beryl quipped, watching as Jez approached the door to the chapel. The students instantly parted to let her through. Even the grownups stepped aside. Jez pushed the door open and entered. As one, the throng massed up behind her and followed her inside.

"Is everybody religious here?" Beryl asked as she and Shōnagon trailed the crowd into the chapel.

"No," said Shōnagon.

"Nothing else to do on Sunday?" Beryl suggested. "Like reading the newspaper?"

"Not exactly," said Shōnagon. "Some kids go to the lake to hang out, some go riding or play soccer or whatever. But nobody does anything until after church. They don't want to miss it."

"Why?" Beryl asked.

Shōnagon grinned at her.

"You'll see," she teased.

Inside, everyone crowded into the narrow pews, their bodies crammed shoulder to shoulder. By the time she and Shōnagon entered, it was standing room only. She searched the crowd for Mr. Lark, but he wasn't among the congregants.

A low buzz of conversation continued for some time. Then, without any sign as to why they were doing so, Medusa, Hecate, and Circe stood up and began to clap out a slow, steady rhythm. The crowd immediately emulated them. This continued for several minutes.

Just when Beryl was beginning to question their—and her—sanity, Jez suddenly leaped onto the low platform that served as an altar. It was such an energetic, animalistic spring that Beryl sucked in her breath in surprise.

"I'm here to talk about the *LORD*! And the fire, the fire eternal, the fire from *BELOW*! That fire, that fire which **BURNS**!" Jez boomed. Her accent had transformed into unadulterated Deep South. Her voice was so bombastic, so theatrical that a giggle of shock instinctively bubbled in Beryl's chest.

The giggle died in her throat, however, as she watched Jez pace the stage, stalking back and forth like a caged lioness. She made eye contact with each person in the chapel as she poured forth a Pentecostal sermon that mounted in intensity, increased in fervor, and distended in unfeigned zeal. Her cadence was hypnotic. It wasn't soothing by any stretch, but it was…bewitching. Her performance—for that's clearly what it was—was polished, professional, and so mesmerizing that Beryl couldn't take her eyes off her.

Shōnagon leaned over and gave her a poke in the ribs.

"See?" she gloated under her breath. "Everyone comes for the entertainment. Christians, Muslims, Hindus, Jews. Even the atheists. She does this every Sunday."

"Who is she?" Beryl whispered.

"Nobody knows," Shōnagon whispered back. "But my old roommate, the one who left me all the hair stuff, she was here when Jez arrived. She told me she'd seen a video of her on YouTube. I think her parents run a mega-church, or something."

"Can you call upon His name? Will you call upon it? Will you call upon it right now?" Jez chanted, and Beryl suddenly realized that she had been sitting stock-still, her eyes half-focused and riveted upon the leader of the God Squad, for nearly half an hour. She shook herself and looked around. Everyone in the chapel was rapt and motionless, staring at Jez.

This girl was hypnotic. Dangerously hypnotic.

Then Beryl had a thought.

If all the students were here, that meant nobody was at the school.

It was the perfect time to do some strategic snooping.

Beryl leaned over to Shōnagon and whispered, "I have to step outside."

Her friend was so spellbound that she didn't appear to hear.

Beryl slipped through the crowd, cracked the door open, and stole out of the chapel.

The road was deserted. So were the school grounds when she reached them thirty minutes later, wheezing and winded. She wasn't normally fatigued by brisk walks. It had to be the altitude. She paused for a moment at the edge of the sports field to catch her breath and consider her options. In the three days she'd been here, she'd had the run of the library, the dining hall, the classrooms, and the student recreation rooms. All the spaces meant for the underage inhabitants of the school. What she hadn't seen were the adult-only areas: the kitchen, the teachers' lounge, the basement.

"There are all kinds of secret corridors and mysterious rooms," Shōnagon had said. Now was the time to explore them. She started for the main door leading into the school. Before she could take more than three steps, it swung open.

Out stepped the headmistress.

She was dressed in hunting tweeds, jodhpurs, and Wellington boots. Around her neck hung a pair of binoculars. Tucked under one arm was a small brown book. Beryl ducked behind a small shed that held sports equipment and watched as she made her way past the field and around the back of the school, where she disappeared into the thick brush that grew along the base of the rockface.

Beryl hesitated. She had two options: she could follow the headmistress and try to discover what she was up to, or she could take full advantage of her absence. Namely, she could search her office.

Beryl swallowed, took a tentative step out from behind the shed, and paused. She listened intently. From the undergrowth, she could hear the cracking of twigs and the swish of branches. She took a deep breath and darted toward the school. She dashed through the front door, ran to the west wing, and pounded up the staircase to the third floor.

At the top of the stairs, she stopped, stood perfectly still, and listened.

There was not a sound within the wing, nor a footstep on the stairs below.

The headmistress's office lay dead ahead. The door was closed. Surely it wasn't...

She tried the knob, and to her shock, it was unlocked. The door swung open, the hinges letting out a yowl of complaint that made her wince. She tensed and looked over her shoulder into the hall.

No one.

On tiptoe, she crept inside.

The headmistress's office was dim, lit only by weak sunlight that shone through the window behind her desk. Beryl approached the window, ducked behind one of the green velvet curtains, and peeped out. On the ground below, she could see the headmistress meandering through the brush. She held the binoculars in her right hand and the brown book in her left. Every few steps, she raised the binoculars to her eyes and trained them upon the trees or the roof of the school.

She was birdwatching.

Since she'd left the door to her office unlocked, it must have been an impromptu birding excursion. Perhaps she spotted some rare avian specimen and popped out to get a closer look. She could return at any moment. Beryl didn't have much time.

She surveyed the office. Desk, filing cabinets, a door with an owl engraving on it that led…somewhere.

She tried the door first. Locked.

She moved to the filing cabinets. Each drawer was locked.

The surface of the desk, which had been covered with files and loose papers when she arrived on Thursday, was bare. Just an old-fashioned desk blotter, a cup filled with pens and pencils, and the intercom box.

There were four desk drawers: three small ones on the left, and a large one on the right. She bent down and tried them one by one. Locked, locked, locked…and locked.

She exhaled with frustration. Then an awful thought occurred to her.

The headmistress had placed Beryl's phone in the large desk drawer the day she arrived. That drawer was locked tight. The phone was her ticket out of here. If she couldn't get her hands on it, she was trapped.

Forget the story, forget the Pulitzer Prize, forget Nellie Bly— she needed that phone and she needed it now.

She began to tug desperately on the handle of the drawer, panic flooding her veins. The key. Maybe the key was here somewhere.

She lifted the blotter. Nothing. She turned the cup upside down, spilling pens and pencils everywhere. Nothing. She reached for—

"What are you doing in here?"

A voice, speaking from the open doorway, caused her to freeze. Icy terror paralyzed her entire body.

But it wasn't the headmistress's voice. It was Mr. Lark's.

She let out a tremulous breath, her heart pounding so fast she could scarcely distinguish one beat from another.

"Thank God!" she quavered. "You have to help me."

"You can't be in here," he said, stepping into the room. "Why are you—"

"Listen to me," she said. "I brought a phone with me. I'm supposed to call when I'm ready to leave. But the headmistress confiscated it. It's locked in this drawer."

Mr. Lark shook his head.

"Well, in that case, you're stuck here. There's no internet, no mail service, no phones or radios of any kind. And," he reached out and grasped her wrists gently to put a stop to her frantic yanking on the drawer handle. "Even if you had the phone, it wouldn't do you any good, Margot."

"What? Of course it will! I just need to call—"

"It wouldn't work," he insisted, his eyes filled with compassion. "Cell phones don't work here."

"How the hell do you know that?"

"About a year ago, one of the pilots brought a phone in. Strictly forbidden. It was a major security crisis; you can't imagine the uproar it caused. But ultimately it didn't matter because the phone didn't work. There are no cellular towers around here. None. He couldn't get a signal."

She wrenched her wrists out of his grip and glared at him.

"I didn't bring a cellular phone," she retorted. "I brought a military-grade satellite phone. Solar charged, extremely long battery life. It could sit in that drawer for a year and still work. We planned this very carefully. Not just how to get me in, but how to get me back out. All I have to do is call my publisher and he'll immediately get the senator to summon me back, claiming the scandal has passed. But I need the phone to do it."

Mr. Lark was quiet. His gaze drifted off her to the window.

"Can you..." he said, and his voice was so soft, so like it had been when he was seventeen that it pierced her heart. "Can you get me out, too?"

"What?" she replied, stunned. "I...Ben...the plan was for me. Just me."

"I want out, Margot," he said, leaning close to her, his eyes burning with an urgency she'd never seen in them before. "I want my life back."

"Ben...there's no way, I can't—"

"You have to help me!" he exclaimed, grabbing her by the shoulders. "It's all your fault I'm here!"

"How?" she cried. "How is it my fault?"

He dug his fingers into her flesh. She let out a cry, more of surprise than pain.

"Let go of me!"

"If you don't help me—" he began.

But then—

"What are you doing in here?"

This time, the voice belonged to the headmistress.

Mr. Lark released Beryl. He took a step away from her, then another and another.

"I was…I was on the second floor," he stammered. "Grading papers in my classroom. I heard a noise."

The headmistress stepped into the office. She brushed aside the spilled pencils and pens, and set the book on her desk. Beside it she placed the binoculars. She eyed him, then Beryl.

"I see," she said.

A tight smile formed on her lips. She took him by the elbow and led him to the door.

"Thank you, Mr. Lark. I'll handle this from here."

She shut the door in his face before he could respond.

Beryl held her breath.

The headmistress gestured at the desk.

"Clean up this mess."

With hands that shook despite her best efforts to keep them steady, Beryl righted the cup, gathered up the writing instruments, and deposited them where they belonged. As she did so, her fingers brushed the cover of the book. With a surreptitious glance, she took in the title: *A Record of Birds*.

If it was filled with sightings of Himalayan vultures, that meant they were somewhere between the Indian subcontinent and the Tibetan Plateau. Red-tailed hawks would signify North America. Golden eagles would point to the Swiss Alps. Her fingers itched to flip open the cover and page through it.

"Sit," the headmistress said.

Reluctantly, Beryl abandoned the book and lowered herself onto the uncomfortable chair that stood before the desk. The headmistress strolled to the window, clasped her hands behind her back, and looked out. She was silent for so long that Beryl began to fidget nervously.

"What were you doing in my office?" she inquired at last.

"Nothing," Beryl replied.

It was, of course, the wrong answer. The headmistress's head swiveled sharply on her neck and an irate gleam glittered dangerously in her eyes. Beryl flinched.

"I was just looking around," she said.

The headmistress unclasped her hands and moved to her desk. She planted her palms on its surface and leaned across, her gaze riveted upon Beryl. Beryl shrank in her seat.

"Try again," the headmistress growled.

"I was curious," she admitted.

"About what?" the headmistress asked. Her voice was filled with barely controlled fury.

"I wanted to know..." Beryl twisted her hands in her lap. "Where I am."

"You are safe," the headmistress replied. "Most children are satisfied with that. Why are you so fixated on knowing where you are?"

"I'm scared," Beryl admitted. It was the truth.

The headmistress's expression did not change, but she settled her tweed-clad body into her chair and exhaled slowly.

"Beryl," she said. "I don't think you're being entirely transparent with me. You aren't, are you?"

Beryl said nothing. She forced herself to meet the headmistress's eyes. She felt naked under the older woman's relentless gaze and she shuddered.

"I think," the headmistress said. "That you want to know where you are so you can escape."

Beryl bit the inside of her cheek to keep her lips from trembling.

"You wouldn't be the first to try it," the headmistress said, her mouth spreading in a smile that was cold and menacing. "And like the others, you wouldn't succeed. No one... *no one* can leave this valley until they are sent for. Those children who refuse to accept that fact are moved to a..."

Her smile widened and Beryl's heart stopped.

"A more secure location within the school."

She meant the aviary. Fear—a deep, abiding fear that made her stomach twist and her eyes water—took hold of her.

Nellie Bly's publisher got her out of an asylum, but there's no way he could have gotten her out of a dungeon. And the same went double for Beryl's publisher.

Her time at the school was up. She had to get the hell out as soon as possible.

Chapter 9

Ben always thought the only way he would ever get out of the valley would be if he sprouted wings and flew away. But now, he was feeling something he hadn't felt in seven years.

Hope.

Margot could get him out.

She had to.

She owed it to him. It was her fault he was trapped in this place.

It was her fault his brother was dead.

It haunted him: the ear-shattering boom of the rifle, his brother's face transformed into a wet blur of red, the sickening sound of his body hitting the damp asphalt.

She told him, "Do it."

It was all her fault.

Or was it?

After all these years, in spite of everything that had happened, he still loved her.

He knew in his heart that he would still do anything for her.

The student lounge hummed with the usual Sunday night activities. Some of the kids were playing Trivial Pursuit. Others were engaged in a game of mancala. A few were building an elaborate house of cards on the floor near the fireplace, in which thick yellow flames danced with slender orange ones.

Beryl was sitting by herself in a window seat reading the book of Shelley poems he had given her for class.

He strolled around the room casually, just a teacher monitoring his students. He stopped to compliment Darwin on her adroit capture of three of her opponent's stones. He peered at the growing house of cards. He drifted over to Beryl. He stood surveying the room with his back to her.

"Meet me in the dining hall at midnight," he whispered. "We'll get your phone."

"How?" she whispered back, not looking up from her book.

"Never mind," he murmured. "But you have to get me out, too."

"Ben—" she began.

"Midnight," he repeated under his breath. "I get out with you. Or I won't help."

She was silent for a long time.

"Okay," she finally replied.

Lights out had been called two hours and fifteen minutes ago. Poe had turned off the lamp and they had said good night, but Beryl hadn't closed her eyes for a moment. She couldn't risk falling asleep.

When the illuminated numbers on the bedside clock read "11:45" she quietly threw off her covers, sat up, and placed her feet on the cold floor. She didn't dare dress and take a chance of waking Poe. As silently as possible, she grabbed her shoes, tiptoed to the door, and eased it open. She glanced at her roommate, then slipped out into the hall.

She shut the door soundlessly and crept along the dim hall. Down the wooden staircase she glided in her bare feet, wincing at every creak. When she reached the ground floor, she slipped on her shoes, opened the door leading to the commons, and stealthily exited the south wing.

The night air was breathtakingly cold. Her thin pajamas did nothing to insulate her. She gasped, wrapped her arms around herself, and jogged across the damp grass toward the north wing. Shivering, she yanked the door open and stood rubbing her arms in the dark hallway just outside the library, whose door was ajar. Not a light shone within, but moonlight streamed through the windows, illuminating the shelves of books with a faint silver glow.

She jumped when she heard a noise from within.

It was a cough.

Had the dining hall proven unsafe? Was he waiting for her among the stacks instead?

She took a step toward the door and listened.

She let out a strangled yelp when a strong hand seized her upper arm and dragged her inside.

"I knew you'd show up, baby," a rough masculine voice rumbled. "You kept me waiting almost an hour, though. I'm gonna have to punish you."

"Let go of me!" Beryl cried, struggling.

Her captor loosened his grip enough for her to spin around and face him.

"Electra?" Lord Byron said.

When he recognized Beryl in the moonlight, his face lit up with a lascivious grin.

"Even better," he purred, gathering her to him. "I didn't think that resentful bitch would show, but I had to take a shot, right? For old time's sake."

"Let go of me, I said!" Beryl ordered, thrashing in his arms.

"No more teasing," he chided, clamping a hand over her mouth to silence her cries. "I know your friends don't like me. Don't worry, I won't tell them."

He smiled, and with an ease that indicated he'd done this before, he scooped her up like a bride and carried her deep into the library, to one of the low-backed couches that stood near the study carrels.

The instant he laid her down, she kicked him squarely in the jaw. He let out a cry of pain and recoiled.

"What the hell!?" he bellowed, clapping a hand to his face. "Why did you do that?"

"I'm not about to be raped by a kid!" she said, leaping to her feet. He seized hold of her wrist.

"I'm not a fucking rapist, Beryl!" he exclaimed, rubbing his jaw with his free hand.

"You're doing a great imitation of one," she retorted, fighting to free her wrist from his grasp. "I know all about you."

"And I know all about you," he said, reeling her in and wrapping his arms around her. She gasped as her back was crushed against his muscular chest. She struggled but she couldn't break away.

"Let go of me!"

"I know you like older men," he whispered, holding her tight. "And I know about you and Mr. Lark."

Instantly her struggles ceased.

"What do you mean?" she asked in a faint voice.

He reached up and smoothed her hair away from her face. He pressed his lips gently to her ear.

"I saw you," he murmured. "Down at the lake Friday night. I saw the two of you kissing. And I heard what you said."

"What did I say?" she whispered, her body going weak.

"Mr. Lark said…" he kissed her temple, then her neck. "'Did you have sex with him?' Meaning me."

"Meaning you?" she repeated, a note of incredulity piercing the anxiety in her voice.

"And you said…" he slid his hand to the top button of her pajama shirt and undid it. "'What the hell is wrong with you?' There's plenty wrong with that possessive asshole. You can do much better."

He nuzzled the nape of her neck.

"That's all you heard?" she asked.

"It's enough, isn't it?" he said, caressing her bare shoulder. "You both could get in so much trouble. I'll keep your secret. But you have to be very, very nice to me."

"Okay," she said. "I'll be nice to you."

He loosened his grip. She rotated in his arms so she could face him. She gazed up at him.

"I'm going to very nicely warn you that if you don't get out of here right now, I'll ruin your life."

His satisfied grin vanished.

"What do you mean?" he said.

"You know that thing you always say? 'Do you know who my father is?' Not only do I know who your father is, I know who you are, too."

She stood on tiptoe, slipped her arms around his neck, and whispered into his ear, "Logan…Asher…Wyatt. But that's not all. I know about the video on your computer. The one the FBI is so interested in."

He pulled away from her, throwing off her arms. His face was horror-stricken.

"How the fuck do you know about that?" he demanded.

"I bet the Feds would love to lock you up for a long time," she continued. "Too bad they don't know where you are. Not yet."

Lord Byron took a step backward. His hands were shaking.

"You've made a huge mistake—" he began.

"No," she said. "You have. I know who you are. But do you know who I am?"

He stumbled as he took another step back.

"No," he said. "Who are you?"

She smiled coldly, the way the headmistress had smiled at her.

"I told you. I'm the person who can ruin your life," she said. "Stay the hell away from me or I'll do it."

After Lord Byron fled the library, she straightened her rumpled pajamas and rebuttoned her top. She clenched and unclenched her hands. Her body was crackling with adrenaline.

She went into the dining hall. It was empty. She sat down at the nearest table to wait. She didn't have to wait long.

"Sorry," Mr. Lark said, sliding through the half-open door just as she was getting comfortable in her chair. "I was heading over here when I saw Lord Byron running across the commons like a bat out of hell. I had to duck into one of the restrooms. Did anyone see you?"

"No," she lied.

"Good..." he said in a voice that was steady, yet filled with trepidation. "You ready?"

She nodded and rose.

This was it. It had to work. If it didn't, she wasn't sure what she would do.

The west wing was dark and deserted. Beryl and Mr. Lark crept up the stairs to the third floor, then moved silently down the hall. No light shone from beneath the door to the headmistress's office, which was securely closed. Mr. Lark took a deep breath, grasped the knob, and turned it.

It didn't budge.

"Locked," he whispered.

"Shit," Beryl whispered back. "I guess that's to be expected, considering."

"Yeah," Mr. Lark murmured, studying the door. "Luckily, I have a key."

He reached into his pocket, hunched over, and inserted an unbent paper clip into the lock. He began to wiggle the thin piece of metal, his face creased with concentration.

"Are you just hoping for the best? Or do you actually know how to pick locks?"

"Well…" he said. Then, with a grin, he turned the knob and opened the door.

"Where'd you learn to do that?" she marveled.

"I was one of Scandal School's best students."

They entered the office, shut the door softly behind them, and crossed to the desk. They didn't dare turn on a light. Through the unshaded window, the moonlight illuminated the filing cabinets, the desk, and the mysterious door with its owl engraving. The rest of the room was cast in deep shadows.

"Where did she put your phone?" he asked.

"In that drawer," Beryl replied, pointing at the largest of the four.

"I suppose it's too much to hope…" he said, giving the handle a tug. "Damn. A flashlight would be a godsend right now."

He knelt on the old rug and inserted the paper clip into the lock.

"These are the worst…" he grunted, twisting the scrap of steel this way and that. "Keep watch, this might take a minute…"

Beryl started for the door to the hall when her eyes fell upon a small brown rectangle just visible in the moonlight that spilled across the desk.

It was a book.

She leaned closer to it. She could just make out the title in the dim light.

A Record of Birds.

It was the book that might—just might—hold the key to the school's secret location.

She reached for it.

"Got it!"

Mr. Lark pulled the drawer open. Beryl withdrew her hand, darted around the desk, and peered into the drawer. Dozens of phones were scattered pell-mell within.

Which of them was hers?

She reached into the drawer and began pulling out phones. iPhones, Samsungs, LGs, and Motorolas. Xiaomis, Kyoceras, Vivos, and Huaweis. Knock-off burner phones. Models with no brand identification at all. The phones got more outdated the deeper she went. She hadn't handled the satellite phone much before the headmistress took it away from her. There'd been just a quick primer on which buttons did what, courtesy of a dour aide to the senator whose machinations got her into this school.

At last, her fingers closed around a bright yellow phone with a blocky body topped by an antenna thicker than her thumb.

"I think this is it," she said, holding it up to the window to get a better look in the moonlight.

"Are you sure?" Mr. Lark asked.

"Pretty su—"

Suddenly she heard a sound from behind the enigmatic door beside the window. A bump. She froze.

"Shh!" she whispered. "Did you hear that?"

Mr. Lark tensed.

"I—" he began, then there was a heavy thump, as if something within the closet or room that lay behind the door had fallen against it, causing the owl engraving to visibly jounce.

Mr. Lark shoved the drawer closed and twisted the paper clip violently to re-lock it.

"Go! Hurry!" he hissed.

Clutching the phone to her chest, she darted for the door. There was no time to grab the birdwatching book or even look behind her to see if they were being pursued. Mr. Lark hurtled into the hall after her, shut the door, jammed the paper clip into the lock, and jiggled it until they heard a faint click. Then the two of them sprinted through the dark hallway.

Down the staircase they dashed.

"Where?" she panted.

"The gym!"

He grabbed her hand and hauled her through the door to the gymnasium. He shoved it closed and leaned against it, listening.

After a moment, he stood up straight and his breathing slowed.

"I think we're okay," he said.

The gym was nearly pitch black, save for a line of green safety lights stretching along all four walls, ten feet above the floor. Their every movement echoed in the vast space. She stared down at the phone.

"Here goes."

She pressed the power button. The screen flashed, then illuminated, glowing like a beacon in the dark. The battery was still fully charged. She pressed the series of numbers that she'd drilled into her memory, then hit the green send button.

Nothing happened.

A message flashed on the small screen.

No satellite signal.

"Shit," she said. She pressed the disconnect button and dialed again.

No satellite signal.

"Shit, shit!"

"It's not working?" Mr. Lark asked.

"No," she moaned. "I don't know what's wrong. I tested it back home. It worked fine."

She hung up and dialed again.

No satellite signal.

Despair washed over her like a wave of frigid seawater. Did this mean she was trapped here?

Why was there no satellite signal?

Of course!

"Satellite phones don't work indoors!" she exclaimed. "We need a clear line of sight to the sky."

"You mean we have to go outside?" he asked.

"Yeah."

"We can't," he said. "It's after curfew."

"There's no other way. If we wait until morning, someone will see us for sure."

"As long as we stay on school grounds, we might be safe." Mr. Lark mused. "Maybe if we go into the woods behind the horse stables—"

She shook her head.

"There can't be anything between us and the telecom satellites in orbit. No brush, no tree branches."

He let out a shaky puff of air.

"Okay," he said. "If we get caught, if someone overhears us…"

"I know," she said.

The sky above the sports field was spattered with stars: it looked as if an enormous bottle of glitter had been shaken over a black velvet cape. They jogged to the soccer goal post at the far end; still the school grounds, but only barely. The air was cold. As soon as they came to a stop, she began to shiver in her thin pajamas. Her hands shook so hard that she had trouble holding the phone steady enough to dial. Without a word, Mr. Lark shrugged out of his tweed jacket and draped it over her shoulders. The thick cloth was warm from his body heat. She gave him a grateful smile and punched in the international dialing number that had been assigned to Baz.

She let out a cry of triumph.

"It's ringing!" she proclaimed.

Mr. Lark stood close to her, his head swiveling from side to side, keeping watch.

"Still ringing," she reported.

"You said you came here because of a boy."

"Logan Asher Wyatt," she replied. "Pick up, Baz. Come on…"

"Do you know which boy he is?"

She nodded.

"Well?"

"I think you can guess," she said.

He thought for a moment, then his face contorted with pure loathing.

"Lord Byron," he growled. "That little bastard!"

"God, pick up, Baz!" she murmured. "Where are you?"

She had no idea what time it was back in Washington, D.C., where *Scandalicious News* was headquartered. It could be the middle of the night. Baz might be asleep. It could be the middle of the day. Baz might be passed out drunk. Or worse. It could be that he'd forgotten all about her. That would be just like him. Distracted by a shiny new scandal.

On the ninth ring, the call abruptly connected and his hearty voice bellowed, "Nellie Bly!"

Relief flowed through her veins like warm liquor.

"Baz! Thank God. Forget the code name, okay? I've already got a fake name, I can't keep track of another."

"Is that right? What is it?"

"Beryl."

"Barrel?" he repeated. "Like what they age the good whiskey in?"

"No, Beryl," she enunciated. "It's a type of—it doesn't matter. Listen: I did it. I'm in. They think I'm seventeen. I've been going to class and everything. I'm flunking math. I don't know where I am. Not even which continent I'm on. The school's hidden in a valley. No roads in or out. There's an airstrip, there's a tiny town, it's insane."

"Too right, it's insane!" Baz agreed.

"There are fifty-three kids here. Plus me."

"Fifty-three kids," he echoed. "Fifty-three innocent children, trapped in a hellish nightmare of a prison. Good on ya, girl!"

"It isn't exactly a nightmare prison," she said, then she remembered the aviary. "But there's a rumor some dangerous kids are locked up somewhere on the grounds. Rapists, murderers, that sort of thing."

"Killer kids, juvenile sexual perverts! Ha-ha! I love it!"

"I've got everything I need to write the story," she said. "I'm ready to come back."

Baz was silent for so long that Beryl feared the call had disconnected.

"Baz? Baz, are you there?"

"Tell you what...I want you to stay embedded at the school," he said.

"What?" Beryl said. "You're joking. That's not funny!"

"Listen here: this started out as just another scandal story, right? But by crikey, this is a bloody scandal goldmine! That school, it's choc a bloc with stories! Think about it, my girl: million-dollar ad sales, bestseller book deals, enough social and political leverage to last for decades, and for you, a job with any journalism outlet you want. Online, TV, magazines, newspapers, in the U.S. or abroad. Take your pick, I'll make it happen."

"Baz, no…" she protested.

But his words resounded within her like a war drum.

It was exactly what she'd wanted all her life. A real job as a real journalist. It could be hers. All she had to do was say yes. Plus, to her dismay, she could feel her heart thudding with excitement, just as Baz's surely was. She longed to reveal rumors. She loved to uncover secrets. This was her biggest flaw, the one she refused to acknowledge. She couldn't resist a good scandal.

"Get cozy with the kids. Find out who they are, what they did, and who they did it to. And Margot?"

"Yeah?"

"I want you to learn everything about that school: where it is, who runs it, how it's funded, everything."

"I guess I have no choice," she said.

"Good girl!" Baz crowed. "You won't regret this."

"I already do," she replied.

"Call me when you have another story," he said.

"Okay."

She hung up.

She stood very still.

"Well?" Mr. Lark said.

She shook her head, her face stricken.

"We're not getting out," she said. "My boss wants me to stay."

"What?" he said.

"It's an important story. Maybe the story of the century."

"So what?" he exclaimed. "Who cares about the story? This is our lives, Margot! Did you fight for us at all?"

"Nobody fights Baz Bennigan and wins," she said. "He wants

118

the whole story. Then we can leave."

"And you agreed to that?"

She shrugged.

"What is it?" he said, coming closer and peering down into her face. "What aren't you telling me, Margot?"

"After it's over, he promised he'll get me hired anywhere I want."

"And how exactly will he do that?" he demanded.

She looked up at him, a bleak expression on her face.

"Leverage. Blackmail. Scandals. The usual."

He shook his head in disgust. He took a few steps away, his hands on his hips. When he turned back to her, his eyes were as cold and hard as stone.

"Just how long do you think you'll be stuck here?" he asked.

"I don't know."

A bitter laugh escaped his lips.

"Welcome to the club."

Chapter 10

Scandalicious News
Publisher Announcement: Big, Big, BIG NEWS!

By Baz Bennigan

Ladies and gents, *Scandalicious News* is embarking upon a daring new endeavor!

An extremely confidential source is risking life and limb for an **EXCLUSIVE SCOOP,** the details of which are soon to be revealed!

Our anonymous source will bring you **ALL THE JUICY DETAILS** about **NAUGHTY ACTS, CRIMES OF PASSION, TRUE GOSSIP, SECRETS** and **SCANDALS** the likes of which you've never imagined!

Stay tuned for our next story! We guarantee it'll be a stunner!

The Monday morning sun peeped over the edge of the eastern rockface, greeting Beryl with thick, bright rays that shimmered across the floor of her dorm room.

She hadn't slept a wink.

She showered and dressed. She executed a few half-hearted stretches. She rubbed her hands over her face, trying to revitalize herself—or at least erase the dark circles under her eyes.

"Want to go to breakfast together?" she asked Poe, who was combing their hair vigorously in the mirror.

Poe grunted neutrally, gave their hair a final swipe, and laid their comb on their dresser.

"I hope they haven't run out of birchermüesli," they said. "That's the only thing I want."

"I just wish they served coffee," Beryl commented, opening the door.

Out in the hall, on the floor just outside their room, stood a brown leather school satchel.

"Whose is this?" Beryl asked, giving it a poke with the toe of her shoe.

"Yours," Poe replied. "It's your school bag. I don't know why it took so long to get delivered."

Beryl bent down and unfastened the brass buckles that held the bag closed. The spicy scent of fine leather pricked her nostrils. Inside were five notebooks bearing the school crest, five sharpened pencils, and two fountain pens. She sank back on her heels and let out a sigh.

"I guess I really am here to stay," she said.

In history and geography, she correctly identified both the dates of the Liberian civil war and the location of the country on a map. "Very good, Beryl," said Mr. Crane. "But we've moved on to Libya. Do you happen to know where *that* is?"

In science, she just shook her head at Ms. Starling. "I don't know a thing about physics," she said. "Not a single, solitary thing."

In math class, she handed in another blank quiz. "Mr. Partridge," she replied, when he launched into a tirade about her deficiencies in the mathematical arts. "I promise you that I will never, *ever* need to know calculus."

In gym, she irritably informed Mr. Cassowary that her stamina would improve once she'd acclimated to the high-altitude air of the valley. "Which should happen around when it's time for me to leave," she snapped.

In the final class of the day, language and literature, she arrived to discover that Mr. Lark had shaved his beard off. As the students got settled in their seats, they peeped at him and tittered amongst themselves until he said, "What? Why are you all so giggly today?"

"Mr. Lark, you have removed your whiskers," said Saint Augustine.

"Change is good," he replied, and his eyes met Beryl's. "Everybody can change."

She smiled sadly at him. He had changed, that was true. He'd changed back. Now he looked exactly like the boy she had known.

The boy she had loved.

"Beryl," he said.

She jumped. She'd been staring at him. She had to break herself of this habit if she was going to survive here.

"Your essay on Shelley's 'To a Skylark,'" he said, holding up the duo of typed pages she'd submitted on Friday. "Excellent work. Your typing leaves a lot to be desired, but the content was superb."

"Thank you," she said.

"You should consider joining the newspaper club," he commented.

She couldn't read the message in his eyes. But he was trying to tell her something. She glanced away and the hair on the back of her neck tingled. She could feel someone's eyes on her. She looked up. The student seated two desks over was staring directly at her.

Poe.

Their observant eyes narrowed slightly. Beryl looked away.

Mr. Lark cleared his throat.

"All right, people. New week, new subject: ancient Babylonian literature."

The class groaned.

He held up his hands.

"Hold on, give it a chance. I think you'll find this fascinating."

An hour later class ended and the students, utterly unfascinated, eagerly rose to exit.

"Beryl," he called out as she headed for the door. "Would you stay behind a moment, please?"

"Um," she said. "Okay."

She retraced her steps. As she passed Poe, her roommate gave her a look.

She approached his desk. The classroom was empty now. They

were alone.

"What are you doing?" she demanded, her words emerging as an apprehensive whisper.

"This isn't about that," he replied, not lowering his voice. "I'd like you to join the newspaper club."

"What?" she said. "Why?"

"I need a good journalist. My current editor-in-chief is fourteen and my proofreader barely speaks English."

She giggled.

"I've met them. They're not that bad," she said.

"You're right," he replied, and now he did lower his voice. "But it will give us a cover story. An excuse to talk."

An excuse to talk.

This wasn't going away. The feelings they shared.

She should say no. What they needed to do was avoid each other. That was the safest course of action.

"All right," she heard herself answer.

"Welcome to the club," he said, repeating his words from last night. This time, there was no bitterness in his voice. He smiled at her. In spite of herself, she smiled back.

The spark was still there. The embers of the fire that had burned between them when they were young. Maybe it wouldn't be so bad being stuck here for a little longer.

His next words were like a bucket of ice water dashed over her.

"But," he said. "You'd better pray nobody finds out you're not who you say you are. They'll never let you leave. Just like me."

He eyed her grimly for a moment, then turned away to sort through the papers on his desk.

"Newspaper club meets here tonight at seven. See you then?"

Stiffly she nodded, and without another word, she hurried out of the classroom.

She drifted down the staircase to the ground floor. She went outside onto the commons. The sun was on the other side of the valley now, hovering at the jagged top of the rockface behind the school. Gathered on the grass were her classmates, all of them talking, laughing, acting like regular teenagers. She was going to have to start acting like a regular teenager herself from now on.

She approached Amethyst and Garnet, her mind abuzz with adolescent small talk she could deploy. As the girls greeted her, a tall, dark figure crossed the lawn just behind them, casting a shadow over their cheerful group.

Lord Byron.

He walked slowly past them. His eyes were locked on her face. The naked malevolence in his glare astonished her.

She shuddered. It was clear that she had made a dangerous enemy.

She felt genuinely frightened.

Poe knocked on the door to the headmistress's office. From within, the familiar voice called out, "Come in." Poe steeled themself and turned the knob.

The headmistress was standing at the window, her back to the door.

"Yes?" she said, without turning around.

"You asked me to keep an eye on Beryl," Poe said. "I saw some things. I think I should tell you about them."

"Mmm?" the headmistress replied.

She wasn't listening. She was staring out the window as if enthralled.

Poe joined her and looked out. There was nothing to see but the sunny afternoon sky, the white-topped mountains, and a bunch of kids milling around on the green grass of the commons.

"What are you looking at?"

The headmistress tapped a blood-red nail against the windowpane.

"Lord Byron doesn't know it, but this time he won't be leaving our school."

"Why not?" Poe asked.

"He's incorrigible," she replied. "And I heard his voice from the Outside."

"I don't understand."

"He talked about the school. He talked to the press. You know what that means."

Poe considered this. They didn't say anything for a long moment. Then they ventured, "Am I incorrigible?"

The headmistress turned away from the window and regarded Poe. The expression in her dark eyes was almost fond.

"Like I've always told you, you're one of a kind," she replied.

"Will I ever leave?" Poe asked.

The headmistress just smiled at them.

"Why would you ever want to leave?"

She moved away from the window, her hands still clasped behind her back.

"Lord Byron," she mused. "That's one little bird whose wings I will be delighted to clip."

She was in a good mood. It was the perfect moment to tell her everything: that Beryl and Mr. Lark knew each other from the Outside. That the two of them couldn't keep their eyes off each other. That Beryl wasn't who she said she was.

Poe opened their mouth to speak.

Then they slowly closed it.

Better to keep it a secret.

Better to keep it for leverage.

At least, for now…

Will Poe expose Beryl's identity? Will Beryl discover the secret of Lord Byron's scandal? And will Mr. Lark's shocking past return to destroy him—and the girl he loves? Find out in Scandal School #2, **TEACHER'S PET**.

Want to be the first to read all the Scandal School books? Join Cat Cavaleri's ARC team: subscribepage.com/arcs

About the Author

Cat Cavaleri writes romance stories you can believe in. From sweet and sensual to steamy and sexy, she loves coming up with unforgettable characters and tantalizing scenes that will fuel your hottest fantasies. Check out her latest books at catcavaleri.com.

Connect with Cat on Twitter or Instagram: @catcavaleri

Subscribe to Cat's newsletter and get a FREE ebook: **subscribepage.com/catcavaleri**